Originally from Hythe, Kent, Graham moved to Scotland's north-east almost forty years ago. There, working in the field of information management, he has been director of library and computing services at the University of Aberdeen and a director of the Digital Curation Centre at the University of Edinburgh.

A wee flagerie for the folk of Newburgh.

Graham Pryor

MAN WITH A GUN

AUSTIN MACAULEY PUBLISHERS™

LONDON • CAMBRIDGE • NEW YORK • SHARJAH

Copyright © Graham Pryor 2023

The right of Graham Pryor to be identified as author of this work has been asserted by the author in accordance with sections 77 and 78 of the Copyright, Designs and Patents Act 1988.

All rights reserved. No part of this publication may be reproduced, stored in a retrieval system, or transmitted in any form or by any means, electronic, mechanical, photocopying, recording, or otherwise, without the prior permission of the publishers.

Any person who commits any unauthorised act in relation to this publication may be liable to criminal prosecution and civil claims for damages.

This is a work of fiction. Names, characters, businesses, places, events, locales, and incidents are either the products of the author's imagination or used in a fictitious manner. Any resemblance to actual persons, living or dead, or actual events is purely coincidental.

A CIP catalogue record for this title is available from the British Library.

ISBN 9781035815661 (Paperback)
ISBN 9781035815678 (ePub e-book)

www.austinmacauley.com

First Published 2023
Austin Macauley Publishers Ltd®
1 Canada Square
Canary Wharf
London
E14 5AA

Table of Contents

1	10
2	23
3	43
4	51
5	62
6	79
7	92
8	110
9	119
10	137
11	149
12	164
13	175
14	184
15	190
16	206

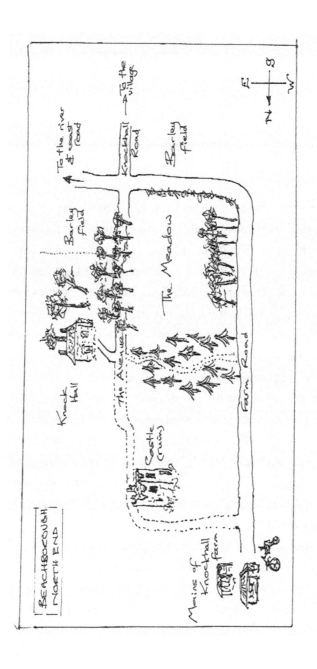

1

If anybody challenged me, I'd freely admit I was responsible for my father's death. But I committed no crime, I assure you.

Of recent memories of him, it was Christmas day two years ago that I still recall with the greatest fondness. When the knock came on his front door, he'd have been expecting to find me standing on the top step. It was a tradition, him opening the door to greet me with a festive glass of negroni in his fist. Of course, finding two well-finished twenty-somethings smiling at him would have come as something of a surprise, I doubt the old misanthrope had even passed the time of day with a tasty young woman for a decade or two. Anyway, the slim blonde accepted the drink from him and shared a sip with her dark companion, before passing him the half-empty glass and, with her arm around his waist, ushered him inside. Well, so it was related to me after his funeral by the two prostitutes.

His heart gave out after his third orgasm. For an eighty-two-year-old with a donor kidney and hypertension, I'm proud how long he'd lasted. But I was already confident the two whores I'd hired were very adept at reviving a moribund libido. I'd been a satisfied client of theirs myself for the past year. It must have been about sixteen years since he'd last enjoyed penetrative sex but both girls confided that everything had been in working order.

I was so very pleased to know he'd died with a big grin on his face. A satisfied smile remained even when he'd been laid out in his coffin, wearing his best chalk-stripe suit. He remained joyful even in death.

So it is these two years later that I still regard my final Christmas present to my beloved dad to be the best five hundred pounds I've ever spent. It wasn't murder I'd committed, in fact it wasn't really death at all. I'd engineered a resurrection.

He left me his gun, a German-made pistol with a twelve-shot clip. I say he left it me but he didn't really, not consciously like. He kept it in the drawer of the old Singer sewing machine that stood in the corner of the living room, the left-hand drawer where my mum, bless her, had kept all her cottons and sewing knick-knacks when she was alive. The right-hand drawer was where he'd stashed a box of bullets, together with a brace of passports, all his. He knew I knew these treasures were kept there and he never moved them, so I'm not fantasising completely when I claim he left them for me.

I take the gun with me now, whenever I go for a walk. I'd certainly go about tooled up if I lived in a city, places like Manchester, Liverpool and Glasgow, where the night streets are ruled by scum. Daytime too, I understand. I was on a plane once, coming back from Heathrow to Aberdeen, when the pilot came onto the radio to tell us we were making good progress. "Those passengers on the left-hand side of the plane," he said, "if you look out the window, you can see Liverpool below. Hold on to your wallets!" I suppose he couldn't say such a thing any more, what with us all being woke nowadays.

Anyway, I don't live in a city but in a village up the coast from Aberdeen. It was a nice quiet place when we moved here, forty years ago, but when we had that pandemic in 2020, folk were encouraged to get outside for exercise, and they started to come out from the city to our beach in huge numbers, for it is indeed a glorious place. Unfortunately, they got the bug for it, not the pandemic bug, that is, but a taste for the outdoors, and the bastards are still coming. Weekends it's hopeless even to think about going for a walk on the beach with the dog, there's scarcely space to move, and these people are always complaining about there being a dog off the lead. Christ, I don't moan about their horrible kids running amok and leaving their trash in the dunes.

So it is at weekends that me and the dog, Sniffer, go on other walks, up and around the quiet lanes behind the village. They are much favoured by the village folk as a peaceful place to walk. There's a lot of birdlife and blossom on the trees in the spring, wild berries and sloes in autumn, you might even see deer there if you're lucky. Sniffer, he's more interested in the pheasants that creep through the barley fields, and once he's off chasing them there's nothing I can do but wait, his nose being his true master. But he always comes back to me eventually, he knows who'll give him his dinner.

But I've wandered away from the point I was going to make, which was about taking the gun on walks with me. You see, as well as the morons who come to gawp at the seals on the beach, we have had less innocent visitors coming out from the city in recent times, not to mention the travellers, whose number seems to have increased since a new reserved site was opened for them nearby. Our village these days is blessed with burglars, twockers, dognappers, doorstep scammers (this last lot typically offering to tarmac your drive or clean your roof), along with myriad other assorted n'er-do-wells, and scarcely a week passes before there's one incident or another reported on the local Facebook page. Fortunately these scoundrels are usually easy to identify. Others are less obvious. Goodness me, I must be making you think I live in a place resembling the Wild West. It's actually nothing of the sort. Not yet, anyway.

There, I've wandered again. So here's where I meant to be taking you, an example of the 'less obvious' villain. Some weeks past, it was a Sunday, I do recall that, I was walking up the lane from the main road that runs alongside the river. I'd let Sniffer off the lead once we were away from the main road, which has become a real racetrack since they built a load of new estates up towards Peterhead, and it seems that everyone who lives there thinks he or she's a Lewis Hamilton once sat behind the wheel. But I digress, sorry. To continue: the lane runs uphill through barley fields to a crossroads, with the left turn leading back to the rear of the village, and the right into a straight stretch that takes you up to a rather attractive old country house (we call that bit of road The Avenue, it's lined with rather fine old trees and there's always a super show of spring flowers every year). Straight ahead over the crossroads, the road goes round a right bend after a short distance, then continues on through more country, past a house on the left where they keep hens, and all the way up the length of another cereal crop to a farm, the Mains of Knockhall. It used to be possible to walk on through the farm to the next village, but a gate has been erected across the top

13

of the road, making it effectively a dead end. Still, if I was a farmer I wouldn't want strangers traipsing through my farmyard, scaring my dogs and nicking stuff, so the gate don't bother me.

Anyway, I was walking up the lane, watching Sniffer slip through the fence to go after pheasants he'd detected lurking in the barley, when there came an ugly roar from behind me and one of them souped up cars with the horizontal wing thing across the back, to make it look like a racing car I suppose, swung in from the main road to come storming up the hill. The lane is only wide enough for a single vehicle, as the tyre prints in the mud on each side attest, and caution is advised. But there was no caution here and, glad that Sniffer was safely off in the barley, I jumped aside as the car shot past. There was some kid driving, some ape with a shaved head, and I caught the number plate. I wouldn't forget that car, a brutal yellow thing with an exhaust pipe wide enough to transport crude oil.

Well, you'd think that was enough excitement for one afternoon, but I'd still not reached the crossroads when I became aware of another vehicle steaming up the lane behind me. Sniffer had abandoned his quest for wildfowl and was examining a small deposit of deer poo by the side of the road. I called him to me as the car sped towards us, but he was entranced by the deer aroma and was taking his time to respond. The car wasn't slowing and didn't slow till it reached us. I stepped back from the road but Sniffer was flung into the bushes. I didn't know if the car had hit him or whether he just realised it was time to scarper in the very last second, though I couldn't find any damage to him later.

The car, a nice clean Audi, had screeched to a halt. It was a woman driving, a po-faced bint with a fancy hair-do. She rolled down her window and gave me a look that said, "This man is a country low-life, one of the little people."

"May I ask where you are going?" I said in my pleasantest of tones.

"None of your business, teuchter," she snapped. "And keep your filthy mutt on a lead."

"I was only enquiring," I said, still calm and friendly, "because I don't recognise you as someone from hereabouts and you might not know that up ahead this is not a through road."

"Is that so?" said the bitch. "And if it's not a through road what are you doing here? On the way to case some lonely cottage for a robbery are you?"

Sniffer came out of the bushes and walked up to the car, his tail wagging its typical friendly greeting.

"Keep that filthy creature away from my car," she shrieked.

Well, as far as I'm concerned, if a person doesn't like dogs they are no sort of person worth knowing, so I reached in and grabbed her by the hair. It was horribly stiff and sticky and I wanted to puke, but I had something to do here, so I hung on. Unfortunately, her seatbelt kept me from pulling her all the way through the window, she was skinny enough to have made it if there'd been no seatbelt, so I had only her head to play with. She scowled at me and spat, but that didn't deter me from giving the woman her medicine and I slapped each cheek hard, pleased to be letting go of that disgusting lacquered hair. When I had done, she started the engine without a word and revved it so the front wheels spun, then took off at a pace across the crossroads, just missing a tractor coming out of the corner gate.

Sniffer and I turned right, up the Avenue, and moments later, across the grassy field that separates the two roads by a couple of hundred yards, we heard her tearing back down from the farm gate, having spurned then confirmed the invaluable advice I had given her.

I have misled you, I have just realised, I haven't mentioned my gun in regard to this incident. Well, it didn't seem appropriate to bring it out on that occasion. Besides, one has to be extra careful now there is a new police powers law. You may have heard how the fascists at Westminster have made it legal for the cops to stop and search anyone without having any prior cause, this act mainly being aimed at stifling attendance at protest marches; but I'm aware that the fuzz around here might take that to be an excuse to stop anyone they might fancy doing over, a bit of a lark to relieve the boredom of waiting parked in the entrance to a field, hoping to nab a fly tipper.

Well, the bitch with the Audi hasn't reported me yet, and it's been a while now. Perhaps she thought better of her attitude towards me, or maybe she found the drubbing I gave her to be unexpectedly exciting. You never can tell what a woman's really thinking. But that's a whole other story we can come back to later.

More to the point, I bet you're asking by now how it was my father owned a gun in the first place. No, he wasn't a military man who'd sneaked a weapon home after some foreign excursion. In fact, he couldn't stand the military, he thought soldiers were dumbfucks with no moral integrity, people who were prepared to go and kill another man or

16

woman they'd never met, simply on the basis that a politician had branded them an enemy.

So, how did father come to have a gun? As it was clearly not designed for sport I always imagined it was something to do with his business. And that was a mystery too. My brother and I used often to speculate what it was he did for a living; you see he never let on, yet we weren't ever short of a penny or two. First of all, we concluded that he was a drug dealer. Seeing him come home in his snazzy suit, with his big moustache and his red doe-skin attaché case, he looked very much the part. He wasn't against the use of drugs, neither, which added to the portrayal. In fact, he once went on a long weekend to Amsterdam with my brother, when my brother was a teenager that is, which was when they went on a grand tour of the coffee shops and were totally spliffed out together. My mother went along to keep an eye on them and she says they were an absolute disgrace in the Rijksmuseum, falling about laughing at Rembrandt's painting of the Night Watch and asking who was the poof in the middle with the frill.

But we eventually agreed to drop the drug dealer accusation. Our other thoughts were that he could be a spy. A sleeper in fact. We watched a film together once about some geezer in the Cold War, who lived an inconspicuous life as cover, for he was actually a Soviet agent waiting to be 'awoken' and put to some anti-Western intrigue or other. Our suspicions gained ground due to the fact he was always railing against English society, how even after centuries it still laboured under the burden of deference. That's actually why we moved to Scotland, where there is a far greater sense of equality and tolerance than down south. We've never regretted the move, especially in these present times when avarice, mendacity and corruption appear to be the chief characteristics at the heart of the UK government. Of course, if he'd been a real sleeper, he wouldn't have risked giving himself away by voicing such an opinion, doing stuff like referring to England as Xenophobia and sniping at the monarchy.

Nevertheless, we reckoned he had a special radio in the loft, by which means he received instructions and secret data from his handler. Our misgivings were given traction by the fact he wouldn't ever let us accompany him if he went up into the loft to get the Christmas decorations or fetch the holiday luggage, he said we'd tread on the pipework or put a foot though a bedroom ceiling, tired excuses which added to our suspicions. But when the Soviet Union ended in 1991 he was unmoved other than to congratulate the cause of freedom, and since then he has cursed Russia's pseudo-Soviet adventures in Afghanistan and Syria. Good job he's not around to witness their disgusting invasion of Ukraine.

All of which left us none the wiser. He was certainly a busy man, and a successful one we discovered when he died. He had no pension to live on in his later years. Didn't even claim his state pension. But he ran a decent motor car, paid for my brother's house purchase and took frequent interesting holidays in the Greek islands. There was always good food to be had at his house too, and plenty of wine in his cellar.

It was after he was dead and buried—I say buried but he was actually cremated, and his ashes spread around the country walks he'd enjoyed with his dogs—yes, after he died I took it upon myself to clear out the house. I didn't expect to meet many surprises, he'd never been a hoarder, but surprise was indeed a poor description for my emotion when I opened the three large suitcases stored in the loft. (I didn't, by the way, find a secret radio up there.) Three innocuous-looking suitcases, one covered in labels celebrating a Baltic cruise with Holland America, the other two evidently well used, the smaller of this pair decorated with a sticker of the bright blue-and-white Scottish flag. But there were no old holiday clothes inside of them, no long-perished face mask or rubber flip-flops, not even any of those anti-mosquito tablets that never got used and used to languish year after year in the zip-up pocket under the lid. What I did discover, filling me with both cheer and consternation, was twelve million quid in used notes, mainly twenties, but with a peppering of fifties too. In addition, I found a further million and a bit in euros. It took me a weekend to count it all.

You'll note I said my reaction was one of consternation as well as joy. Well, natch, what could one do with this amount of cash without drawing attention to oneself? This is the digital age, mate. Who uses cash these days? It's all card payments and electronic banking now. I didn't for the moment wonder at that time how my old man had amassed such a fortune, not even congratulate myself that we'd probably been right with our drug dealing speculations.

All I could think about now was the conundrum of how I was going to spend it. I first thought about big ticket items, expensive cars, jewellery, that sort of thing, where the right sort of dealer is not going to ask questions about a large cash payment. But that would only nibble at the pile of moola that I had in front of me. The euros I could handle, I'd give my brother and his kids generous wads of spending money for their holidays on the continent, and an animal welfare charity based in Europe that I have sponsored from time to time would not baulk at a sizeable contribution, I was certain.

What worried me too was the possibility of a new version of the two currencies being issued, which would render my hoard worthless unless I could change it at the bank. This last was no option considering the size of the sum I had inherited, a sum of money that for all I knew had highly dodgy origins. Consequently, and with some hesitation, I decided I would have to find some way of laundering it.

I tried to remember what they'd done to launder money in films I'd seen. The most recent was the 'Ozark' series on Netflix. There, they had opened a casino, a place where money flowed like liquid and large sums of a dodgy drug baron's dosh could be legitimately banked as takings. Thinking about 'Ozark', however, drew my mind to the more sinister underbelly of a money laundering operation, the gangsters and hard men who would want an in. Thinking about 'Ozark' is also when I finally began seriously to recall what my brother and me had thought about Dad's business interests. Perhaps this cache in the loft really was drug money. Worse, supposing it was somebody else's drug money? This last thought was probably the main reason why I always carry the gun on me, if you want the truth.

Still, having no experience of casino management, I needed to think of another more inoffensive operation, one with predominantly cash transactions, something that didn't carry the constant fear of being shot, like in 'Ozark'. That's when I hit upon the idea of using Benny's fish, chip and burger bar.

Benny, whose real name is Bernardo, is an ex-con. There's nothing nasty about him, I hasten to add, he didn't

20

mug old ladies or stick broken bottles in the faces of opposing football fans. Bernardo was essentially an entrepreneur, a highly skilled accountant—a creative accountant he always says—who'd spent time in clink for the crime of defalcation (fraud to you and me). Not exactly a heinous crime, the government is doing it all the time, you only have to think of what went on during the pandemic. Anyway, Bernardo was a free-lance accountant contracted to several of the big oil companies working up here. He had this fancy production accounting software he'd written, which enabled him to give his employers advantage from avoiding—no, he says I shouldn't use that word—by finding options for tax exemption, and here we're talking PRT. That is, petroleum revenue tax, which is big numbers I can promise you. His fancy software didn't stop there, it also siphoned off a great deal of money into Bernardo's private offshore accounts, and I'm not talking offshore as in north sea oil platforms! Luckily, when he was rumbled, the companies that had employed him wanted to avoid a big fuss and the consequent adverse publicity, the result being that the evidence presented was limited and Bernardo was put away for just five years.

Once he was freed from prison after two years (good behaviour), Bernardo found himself barred from practising as an accountant, he wasn't even able to sell his story to the papers, who'd been there to meet him when he came through the prison gates, as he'd signed a non-disclosure agreement with his employers. This meant he had to find something new and, as a dyed in the wool entrepreneur, he didn't sit on his backside waiting for opportunities to come to him. After dabbling in a number of ventures, he found something he says he actually enjoys. And so, ta-da, we in the north-east are able to enjoy Benny's Burgers, a suite of half a dozen outlets across the region serving food at a lower price and higher flavour quotient than the big international corporate outlets. Queues for his burgers or fish and chips have become legendary and, during the pandemic, when we were all stuck at home, he branched out into home delivery. All mostly cash transactions, was what came to my mind.

There is another side of his business that is highly successful financially, risky business actually and all solely cash-based. It did cause me a bit of anxiety, the prospect of getting involved with Benny, knowing that his side-line could easily prove a weakness in our arrangement, a point of potential exposure to the authorities, or indeed to any criminal snooper. But I'll come to that in a little while.

2

Benny, who should really be called Bernie, only he abjured that diminutive on account it was the moniker of an American politician he regarded as wrong-headed, well, Benny had been known to me for some years, since he provided advice to my father in his dealings with the Inland Revenue. I discovered that one time when my dad was struggling to do his books, as he called it, and asked me to take a letter from the taxman round to Benny, to see if he could explain what it meant. After that, I was aware of a fairly regular discourse between the two men. It can't have been that they were simply mates, as my old man didn't encourage friendship with anyone, and anyway, there were too many years between them for there to have been much shared interest. (Mention David Bowie to Benny and he'll say 'oh yeah, that dead bloke, song and dance act wasn't he?', whereas my dad was a real fan and was always going on about the Ziggy Stardust tour.)

Dad had only good words for Benny. He said he was a straight kind of guy, and I know he put his trust in him and always acted on his financial advice. Even when he was done for embezzlement Dad stuck to his good opinion, just acknowledging that Benny had been unlucky and that the corporates were the truly bent characters in the whole affair, and deserving to be the victims for once. So it was no stranger I approached when I needed advice on the disposal of my windfall. Given the insight Benny must have had to my dad's business, I wasn't worried either that he'd become suspicious about the source of these riches. He must have known all along.

We met several times, upstairs over his first Benny's Burgers premises. That's when I unexpectedly renewed my acquaintance with Magda and Rula, who'd just started to occupy a flat there. From somewhere in eastern Europe, these were a really tasty twosome who'd come to Scotland to escape rural poverty and, with Benny's help, had started their own business. Magda was a tall slim blonde, whereas Rula was her exact opposite, a rather muscular dark brunette, who looked as though she'd been shoe-horned into her trademark tight skirts. A fitness fanatic, well-toned Rula was down the gym every morning at six, whereas sylph-like Magda preferred a slow bath with coffee and cigarette to ready her for the day. How Benny had met them I never found out, but I put their easy relationship down to the Italian in him.

So, the long and the short of it is that Benny took to my very bald proposal, seriously tweaked by him, of course, in order to map with his own business strategy. "I'm doing this for your papa," he insisted, "for your papa and his family." He laughed, "And to stick it to those bastardi who rule the roost in this country. Che cazzo, let's do it!" Yes, I agreed, fuck 'em. My dad would have applauded the sentiment.

From that point on, I had a partner. I also found I had two new friends in Magda and Rula. I say friends, because that's how I regarded them from then on, for we had already enjoyed a business relationship of a sort, previously, before I discovered their link to Benny. I dare say you'll have guessed by now that these were the dextrous pair who had despatched my father so contentedly, oh lucky man that he was.

I did wonder—out loud, as it happens—whether the money I'd found in the loft might in fact be Benny's spoils from the oil company caper. But no, he assured me, it was all mine by right of inheritance. He had never taken cash anyway; all his ill-gotten gains had been moved into a clutch of offshore accounts purely by electronic means. He was proud of what he'd achieved, he said it made him feel very British, hiding his money in the Seychelles, Cayman Isles and Panama tax havens.

Well, I said we met upstairs in Benny's first burger shop, and the first thing we decided we needed to do was open several more to increase the flow of liquidity through our laundry, like perforating a rose in a watering can. The metaphor became part of our secret language: the stash itself became water, Benny's business software the watering can and the unwitting staff we recruited to run the proliferating burger shops were referred to as the gardeners. As for the girls who populated Benny's lucrative side-line, we called them—don't laugh—the blossoms, and their working premises, one upstairs in each burger shop, were known as the florists. I know, it all reads as pretty crass when it's written down, but so do a lot of best-sellers. Besides, it worked for us. Each girl was given the name of a flower, which was another cover and helped them retain some anonymity.

As I think I've explained, we soon had six outlets, four across the city and two out amongst the rural community. With oil on the decline, we had no trouble recruiting to both sides of the business. I'll just explain the background to

25

Benny's side-line first, it's the more historically educational of the two.

During the North Sea oil boom years of the Seventies and early Eighties, Aberdeen had been quite a wild place. Every year there was an oil convention attracting thousands from all over the globe, and whenever there was an event to celebrate, such as a field coming onstream or a new reserve detected, extravagant parties would be held. My dad told me of one oil major that actually bulldozed flat a piece of council-maintained parkland in front of its offices in order to erect a big marquee. They even restored it afterward. In such an atmosphere, the girls involved in Magda and Rula's business were able to make a tidy sum, for there was no end of drunken gits prepared to part with dosh for a knee-trembler at the back of the marquees. But these days, business has changed and the watchwords are USP and service quality. I could see this in the conditions in which my two friends operated. Their apartment was no IKEA show flat but a real classy boudoir. They were picky about their clientele too (in fact I wonder how I managed to be a client of theirs. Ain't I modest!). The other girls we recruited were more than happy to swap hanging around the port's chilly Market Street in a fur coat and no knickers for a warm, safe and cosy apartment.

Benny's burger bars all had tonight's menu on a blackboard behind the counter, giving a price list for the different burger options and what fish were available on the day. At the bottom was a line referring to the pick of the day, which gave the name of a flower (e.g. Rose or Anemone) and instead of a price said POA (price on application, for those unfamiliar with the term). We'd even have a couple of bunches of the named flower in a display vase on the counter, just to make it look authentic. You'll perhaps recall I said earlier that the queues for Benny's Burgers were legendary, well, the reason may now be other than what you thought at the time. Lots of flower lovers here in the north-east. Hah!

As for our legit operation downstairs, we were able to pick and choose when it came to staffing the shops. There had not only been a downturn in the oil industry, but the local university too was shedding staff. Scotland having been dragged out of the European Union by England, the local university was losing undergraduates aplenty. Whilst in the EU, students from Italy to Estonia had been able to attend as undergraduates on the same fee-free terms as Scottish students, but now they had to pay and were voting with their feet, leaving courses under-subscribed. The consequence for some staff was redundancy and they had scant prospect of picking up academic work elsewhere. It may seem odd to think they'd take a job serving fish and burgers, demeaning even, but Benny paid well and, as they say, any port in a storm. So, what with a handful of linguists and historians, plus a number of sharp-witted administrative staff from big oil, we were blessed with a rather well-qualified team. It was a team that, in addition, was disgruntled enough with 'the system' to happily turn a blind eye to Benny's secondary enterprise.

In fact, one of them, a refugee professor from Communications and Control, suggested his own system of another kind after talking to Rula one afternoon. This prof's suggestion was in response to Rula's distaste at the thought of entertaining men whose looks she found repugnant, which was a fair point. Being a whore doesn't mean you have no values. The solution involved installing a hidden camera at the back of the ground floor shop, so that the girls upstairs could survey the customers and, if a man was asking about the pick of the day, they could speak to the counter staff via an earpiece to say whether or not business could be done. Benny, who's a real people person, thought that was a great idea, and we made it a practice in all of our premises. I've sat behind the counter a few times myself and it's been some education seeing the looks of disappointment when a man has been told sorry, pick of the day is off the menu. I shouldn't laugh really, but we have to think first of the wellbeing of our employees.

Well, to move on, things have been going rather well for over two years now. Benny's take away business has been booming and his floristry enterprise, as he calls it, would be given three Michelin stars if there was such a thing for the sex trade. I recently reckoned that I could have reduced my original stash of sterling notes by half in another eighteen months. As for the euros, I sent off an unmarked package containing half a million to my preferred animal welfare charity, and I was pleased to see they thanked an anonymous donor for a very substantial gift when they issued their annual newsletter.

Thing is, though, I've recently landed myself in a bit of trouble. Thursday afternoon only a little while back I was out with Sniffer, hiking up that lane I described earlier. It was a bright, sunny afternoon and the snowdrops were in full display along the roadside. I felt alert and relaxed at the same time. It was the sense of spring being imminent, I suppose. Sniffer was off rooting out pheasants in the field on my right but I expected him to emerge for a biscuit at the crossroads, where there's an entrance to the field. It's his routine. Well, just as he did just that, having had little success with the pheasants, a white van came up to the crossroads from the left and turned to go down the hill behind me to the main road. I called Sniffer to wait and he sat, but the van didn't move on. Instead, a man got out from the passenger's side and came towards us. He was a youngish type, well-built, with a beard that had a white stripe down the middle and he was wearing a denim jacket and trainers (I dislike both beards and trainers, but that didn't make me immediately hostile). "That's a nice dog," he commented, bending to stroke Sniffer, which was when I saw the white stripe was repeated in the hair on the man's head. Sniffer was his usual friendly self, his tail wagging furiously (*'Expecting a biscuit,'* I thought, *'as always'*). I was wondering, in my usual specious way, whether the white stripe meant the man had been struck by lightning, when, as natural as if it was the accepted thing to do, I saw Stripey clutch Sniffer's collar firmly in one hand and drag him round to the back of the van, his other hand out to open the doors.

"Oy!" I shouted, "you don't do that." I ran forward and Stripey pulled out a long knife.

"Fuck off," he spat, "or get a taste of this."

That's the moment when I remembered I had my dad's gun. So I pulled it out from my coat pocket, slipped off the safety catch, and shot him. Unfortunately, at that exact moment a pheasant in the field entrance gave one of its loudest cackles and rose noisily into the air from where Sniffer had chased it behind a straw bale. Galvanised, Sniffer jerked himself free from the man and took off after the bird, Stripey lurched forward to grab him, and my shot failed to hit its intended mark. Instead of his arm I'd shot him in the knee, that was plain, for he immediately crumpled against the van. I was taking aim again when the driver of the van appeared,

29

gave me a challenging look, and proceeded to drag his mate round to the passenger door. It was the instant when I hesitated. Did I want to shoot two blokes? It seemed a bit OTT, a mite unnecessary.

Whilst I was pondering this conundrum the van's engine started and it began to roll off down the hill. As I watched, a hand shot out from each front window, both driver and passenger giving me the finger. That decided me and I let off three shots at the back of the van, which swerved momentarily then continued on. I watched it recede into the distance until Sniffer reappeared, seemingly untroubled by having been manhandled. We were turning into the Avenue when there came an almighty bang and Sniffer jumped into the brambles. I looked back down the hill to see the van had reached the main road, where it had run into the metal post holding the 30 mph sign and was smothered with smoke, some bright flames just about visible. As I watched, the passenger door opened and a man hopped away on one leg. Then came another, more powerful explosion and the rear doors flew off. One of my shots must have hit something vital, a petrol line or something (I'm not terribly au fait with automobile terminology). I watched the vehicle burn and blacken for a while, just checking it hadn't set fire to the stubble in the field, which would have been dangerous, and hoping there had been no other dogs inside the van, then we were able to continue on our way. We heard the shrill of a fire engine's siren a while later, as we took the turning round by the ruins of Knockhall Castle, or maybe it was an ambulance. Indeed, both vehicles could be seen as we walked back round our circuitous route and arrived once more at the fateful crossroads. But out here, away from the centre of the village, no crowd had gathered.

Some cars could be seen going along the main road, but I spied a policeman hurrying them past the scene. '*Oh, chins will wag,*' I thought, '*back in the village.*' The local Facebook pages will be hot with speculation: '*What was that noise just now? Everybody bring your kids in and lock your doors.*' Well it seemed that only I could tell what had gone on, me and the emergency services, us and a few rubberneckers from Cruden Bay.

As far as I was aware, there had been no witnesses to this confrontation and its aftermath, only the crows on the power lines, so why did I introduce this little tale by saying I'd got myself into a spot of trouble? Well, do you believe in coincidences? I don't usually, and I'm not sure even if this is what you'd call a coincidence, but I was just coming away from the village shop with a litre of milk on the following Sunday when a noisy old Mercedes drew up, one of those big grey 380 SE saloons loved by the folk who tend to go in for bling. A bloke got out the driver's seat and came round to the passenger side carrying a crutch, opened the door and helped out a geezer with a beard, a beard split down the middle by a bright white stripe. This second character flashed a glance at me as he clambered out of his seat, but I still had on my anti-Covid mask (still required in our shops, thank you Nicola) and with luck he didn't recognise me as I hastened along towards home. There was no question, it was Stripey the dognapper. Hot damn!

But luck proved not to have been with me that morning, well not the good variety, and I had the feeling (reinforced by the sound of a dirty motor coming down Main Street) that I was being followed. I didn't look round and I kept my mask on all the way home, and the noise faded away once I turned the final corner. Thing is though, I was out sweeping up leaves during the afternoon, and I'm sure I saw a big grey Merc slide past the end of our cul-de-sac a number of times. I'm sure, I say, or else I'm paranoid.

I told the two girls what had happened when they were discussing security with me the next morning, it seemed oddly apposite. They were telling me how they liked the spy camera set-up but how they could still sometimes find themselves in a sticky situation with an aggressive client who'd passed visual approval.

"Most of them are married men whose wives are passive in bed," explained Magda, "women who never take the initiative, some who lose interest in sex after having produced children and are content just to grow fat and unresponsive. Those men are no bother, they are just seeking the pleasure they once knew with their wives."

"But there are others," interjected Rula, "who see us as a way to live out their fantasies, fantasies that will include the aggressive conquest of women. These miso…miso…"

"Misogynists," prompted Magda.

"These misogynists are guys we have to be careful with, as things can quickly become dangerous." She looked to Magda for approval. Magda had made greater strides with her English.

We talked on, considering different emergency procedures to keep the girls safe. It was also when I confided how at the moment I was feeling under some kind of threat myself. Rula responded with her characteristic hard-headedness, a natural pragmatism I had come to recognise, which had been behind her resolve to escape a life of destitution east of democracy.

"I have been reading about dognappers," she said. "In newspaper. A man in Dyce had his dog lifted from garden and a woman in Kintore was stabbed when she tried to hang on to her Labrador. It is an epidemic."

So, I hadn't experienced an isolated incident, it seemed.

"I help," said Rula in her sometimes choppy English. "I like dogs. I help catch your man with stripe."

I wasn't sure if he was available to be caught. It was probable that his mate, the driver, had been shot and burned to death in the van. Stripey may no longer have the means or inclination to go after people's dogs. Dognapping with an old Mercedes somehow didn't seem practicable. Anyway, the thought of this young woman tackling a couple of thugs had an air of the absurd about it.

"I come stay with you," said Rula. "I make lure and we catch him."

Well, the prospect of Rula staying in my house was thrilling, I admit, but I still did not like the thought of putting her in danger.

"Rubbish!" she exclaimed. "He in danger. I do martial arts." And she leapt into a display of crazy bodily contortions, arms flailing and legs propelling her from the floor to head height. '*Jeez,*' I thought, '*a banshee.*'

"Yes," said Magda. "She good. She kill a man in Belarus. On our journey. A very bad man."

It was enough for me, and Rula came out that evening to meet Sniffer, who she said would be part of her plan.

She disappeared after breakfast the next morning and I heard her moving about upstairs. After half an hour, the sound of her footsteps backwards and forwards on the creaky floor of the landing suggested she was in some kind of trouble, so I crept up the stairs to see. Such was my surprise to find not Rula, but a bent old woman in a headscarf and shapeless dress, making sharp thrusts with her arms and feet at an invisible enemy. A packing case that I had filled with my parents' old clothes, which had long been destined for a charity collection but which I'd never got round to shifting, stood open on the landing.

She saw my look of incredulity and laughed. "It's me, Rula," she gasped. "I sorry," she said, pointing at the packing case. "My disguise." She had also found the walking stick my father had always taken on long walks in the hills and was twirling it like a Karate Bo staff.

I helped her complete the outfit, unearthing a drab coat and an unopened packet of horrible brown tights my mother had left in a drawer. From the bottom of the packing case, I excavated some stoutly sensible women's walking boots.

"We go together first time," she declared. "So I am used to Sniffer and he to me, and to know the route."

I was unenthusiastic. "But I suspect the dognapping 'epidemic' might be over in this area. What I did probably warned them off." It was more my hope than conviction.

Rula wouldn't be convinced. "These are Roma. They never warned off. Not back at home, where there are many, and not here." She was determined and I wondered if there was some personal history driving her.

And so it was, that afternoon, I set off with Sniffer and Rula on my customary circuit of the Knockhall lanes. She leant on my arm like an old lady, and the uncomfortable boots added to her assumed geriatric gait. Instead of the enthralling young Rula I had enjoyed several times it looked as though I'd picked up some withered old bag lady. She kept her head down, her back arched with bogus curvature of the spine, but I could see she was noting all the key features of our route, places where one might be ambushed, spots that were concealed by a bend in the road, passages where a van might have to drive slowly and others that would allow a speedy getaway. She pointed them out to me, features that I had always taken for granted, now viewed through an entirely different lens. She was smart, this beautiful whore.

The walk was uneventful other than for some quizzical looks I received from villagers who knew me. *'Who is this? Perhaps his auntie's come to visit.'* At least, I hope that's what they thought. Being out with this frail old dear on my arm was doing my reputation no good at all.

Well, as I say, the walk was uneventful. So was the one after that and another half dozen walks that followed, which Rula made on her own. With Sniffer, that is.

We were up in my bedroom on a weekend afternoon, playing ride a cock horse, Rula being a bit concerned that so long away from work she'd get out of practice. I was barely within reach of Banbury Cross when we heard a peculiar rattling at the front door. With a look of rue, Rula dismounted and I put on my dressing gown and went downstairs, feeling highly disgruntled at the interruption. I felt a good sight worse than disgruntled when I'd opened the door, for tied to the knocker with wire was the corpse of a young whippet that had had its throat cut. Taped to the door was a filthy piece of paper with the words 'We no were you live' scrawled with a ballpoint pen.

"You see," said Rula, who'd pulled on her pink jumpsuit and joined me. "The epidemic isn't over. And," she continued, examining the dead puppy, "this is defo work of Roma. I seen like it back home. It's a warning."

I think I would have reached that last conclusion by myself, but I had to take her instinct about the Roma on trust. It could easily have been village teenagers on a trip had done this. There is a drugs situation in the village, everyone knows, but the kids usually confine their experiments with sex, drugs and alcohol to the concealment of the dunes. All the same, I've done nothing to antagonise the local youth, so maybe she was right.

I was much less keen to let Rula go walking alone after that.

"But I am lure," she insisted. "They see you, they fuck off quick sharp. They see me, they see easy prey."

But, adamant as she was, I decided I couldn't set her up like bait on a hook and just leave her to it. So I determined to follow her at a discreet distance, my gun in my pocket of course. I also attached a hidden tracker to Sniffer's collar, just in case he was successfully nabbed.

She set out the next afternoon in her old woman's gear, leaning on her walking stick, with me lurking a good way back, but not so far I'd be no help if she was attacked. Sniffer knew I was there and kept turning round, which threatened to upset the whole exercise, but eventually his nose turned to the fascinating scents along the verge. There was a red van parked halfway up the Avenue, which was a bit unusual, but nothing came of it when Rula turned right at the crossroads and headed down towards the river. I caught up with her a little after and in a minute or two we heard the van speed over the crossroads in the direction of the village. I conjectured that it was perhaps connected with the workmen installing new drainage up by the farm, there had been excavators noisily busy for a week now. Or maybe I was just trying to convince myself our problem had evaporated.

So, nothing dramatic to report.

"That was them," said Rula when we were home. "They were up there looking at the house, I promise you. A big old house like that, there will be valuables."

If it was the so-called Roma dognappers, then they would have seen us, both of us, and I just hoped they didn't make the connection. As I wasn't carrying poo bags and a supply of biscuit treats I'd not worn my usual dog walking coat with the big pockets, so perhaps they'd not have recognised me. I resolved to wear some disguise the next time we went out.

We had two further negative perambulations before our trap was sprung. Then, for the second time in a week when we approached the crossroads, there was that red van parked a little way up the Avenue. I was in the field next the road, creeping along under cover of the willows that bordered the road, my boots covered with sheep shit, and I was sweating under the heavy black leather coat and beanie I'd put on for disguise. Even through my dark glasses I could clearly see Rula and Sniffer up ahead. Just a short dash would take me to the field gate in the corner at the crossroads.

The van eased out of the Avenue before I had made it to the gate and created a barrier across the road. Two men got out, neither of them recognisable as Stripey, and approached Rula. I hot-footed it to the gate, still concealed by the big crab-apple tree that leans there, and felt for the gun in my inside pocket.

There was a loud conversation going on between the men and Rula, who was waving her hands at them. I could hear

37

snatches: "We know your game, bitch" and "we ain't gonna be conned by you" were two memorable phrases. I also heard the accusation "you're Old Bill, aintcha?" There was no attempt to snatch Sniffer, but suddenly the men grabbed Rula's arms and pulled her back to the van. "We'll teach you," one of them shouted, "get in the van." He wrenched the back doors open and pulled her by her tightly knotted headscarf. But she held on to her stick, kicked him in the goolies and cracked the stick down hard on the second man's head. She was adopting a kung fu stance when I jumped the gate, she was chopping at the first man's throat, seemingly unperturbed, and I was deciding which of her assailants I should shoot first when the second man pulled out a knife and thrust it at Rula. She spun round, her foot out to kick it away when there came a loud blast from behind and the knifeman jumped in the air, dropping his weapon. He fell backwards and lay motionless while Rula gave elegant straight-hand cuts to the first assailant's neck, who collapsed against the side of the van. I never got to fire my gun, but somebody had shot the knifeman, we could see blood pooling around his shoulders.

Footsteps on the gravel made us look up. It was the elderly woman who lives in the big old quaint house up the top of the Avenue, dressed in her customary dungarees and green wellies. We call her the Duchess on account she is so well-spoken and has several gardeners employed to tend her extensive lawns. She was rather inelegantly carrying a shotgun.

"There," she said, looking down at the bleeding figure on the ground. "About time I dealt with these gyppos, always creeping around my house asking if I want the trees lopping or my walls rebuilt. Thieves, all of them" She sniffed and blew her nose on a clean white handkerchief embroidered with a fleur-de-lis. "I know what they're up to, seeing what they might steal from me. I've already lost some statues from the lawn and someone has stolen my prize chickens."

"So what do we do with these two?" I asked. She looked at the man leaning against the van, gasping for breath, and immediately raised her gun at him.

"Not a good idea. Very satisfying but likely to bring you more trouble."

The man had sat up when threatened with the gun and was looking feverishly for a way of escape.

"Are you the driver?" I asked, and he nodded. "Get in, then. Fuck off and don't come back. None of you."

It took him no time at all to be behind the wheel and racing down the hill.

"What about him?" asked Rula, pointing at the man on the ground, "is he dead?"

A quick examination answered her question. I didn't know whether the chill in my stomach was relief or anxiety.

"We might get away with manslaughter, but shooting in the back like that they'll say it was murder, you know what the authorities are like." I was thinking aloud.

"Pish!" snapped the Duchess. "Get him behind the fence, will you. I will deal with this. We don't need any authorities involved, it is the authorities who brought them here in the first place, setting up a fancy campsite for them along the road. You, young man, you stand guard until I return. Five minutes." She held up her spread fingers and thumb as she set off. Then, turning back, she said, "I know you, but dressed like that you could be taken for a foreign spy. I might have shot you as well. Be warned." Good job she hadn't heard

39

about the legendary radio in my dad's loft—now my loft, of course.

There was no sign of Sniffer, who had headed into the barley field next the Avenue, and we spent the next few minutes calling him. He arrived just as a massive yellow digger rumbled down the avenue, with the Duchess perched on the footplate. "Talley-ho," she called, waving that handkerchief.

"This Englishwoman," said Rula, "she not nice."

"She's not English, just thinks she's posh, part of the gentry in her big house. And why do you reckon…"

"She say gyppo," explained Rula hurriedly. "It not nice. She too haughty." She coughed out the unfamiliar word.

Wow, Rula must be the first woke prostitute I'd encountered. But I suppose in her line of work she has to be openhearted to all and sundry. Would the Duchess class as sundry? I think not. She—the Duchess—was at this moment instructing the driver of the digger and in little time he was excavating a trench beside the drystone wall of the field. A deep trough was quickly engineered and the digger driver scooped up the corpse in the jaws of his machine, depositing it with a thump amongst the exposed roots of a giant ash that grew through the wall from the Avenue.

By the time he'd finished pushing soil into the hole, one would never know what had been concealed there. All anyone could tell from the freshly turned soil was that some agricultural work had been going on.

The Duchess had stood all this while with her arms folded and a tight smile on her wrinkled old face. "Should we say a few words?" I asked, not really meaning it but knowing that Rula was a good catholic. "Not bloody likely," retorted the

40

Duchess, hotly. "I've said my piece. Vermin like that deserve no more."

She stepped closer to me, so close I could smell the mints on her breath. "I assume you can hold your tongue, young man. I know where you live; I knew your father, God rest his soul." She nodded at the digger driver. "Don't worry about him. He works for me. He knows where his bread is buttered."

I didn't answer, just nodded and put Sniffer on the lead.

"Goodbye," said the Duchess. "Enjoy the rest of your walk."

We continued down the hill towards the river.

"She doesn't care, does she?" exclaimed Rula. "It could have been a fox she shot."

"It's called entitlement," I explained. "People like that don't believe the rules apply to them."

"People like what?"

"The nobs."

I spent the walk home puzzling whether my own disregard for rules and regulations made me a candidate for the elite in society. But of course, I concluded, there is a criminal elite as well as the nobs. My next conundrum was to consider what set them apart from each other. Fortunately there was insufficient time to pursue those thoughts for long as we were quickly home once more, and Rula was eager to rehearse her technique before going back to work the next day.

"Do you think we have seen off your dognapping men?" she asked, her cigarette poised dangerously near my pillow. "Only I could ask Magda to take over here so that I can return to business, she's great with a knife."

With regret, I had already concluded that the intervention of the Duchess probably had done the trick. There would be all kinds of fervent conversation going on at the travellers' site, not just about the risks from carrying on their nefarious activities but including fears that they might be evicted, the Duchess being well known to have powerful connections. So tomorrow night I'd be all alone in my bed, with just Sniffer for company. Still, there was yet time for another trip to Banbury Cross.

3

It took me a while to reach Banbury Cross. Whilst my manhood of its own volition kept Rula rocking contentedly on her divine fulcrum, my mind was inconveniently elsewhere, trying to make sense of that phrase the Duchess had thrown at me: 'I knew your father, God rest his soul'. How come, in what way had she known him, and was her sympathetic reference to his soul more than a mere platitude? I know it wasn't the time and place but it niggled at me and I was turning the words over and over, trying without success to connect them with a memory. It was only Rula's breathy plea in my ear—"what's keeping you, honey?"—that snapped me out of it and I urged my steed on to the fabled Cross.

As we lay back and shared a cigarette Rula brought up the subject of the Duchess herself. "That posh woman," she said, "with a trace of venom in her speech, do you know her very well? I mean, I heard her mention having known your father."

"First I heard of it," I admitted, and it truly was. I'd combed through my memory of childhood conversations with my father, frugal though they were, and nothing sprung out at me. It seemed unlikely anyway, he was not fond of old money; he would have disdained a woman who invited the little people in the village every spring to bring their children

43

to pick daffodils from her lawn. Lady Bountiful, he'd have called her.

"Do you have her name?" pressed Rula. "Is she nobility?"

"Mrs Delacroix? No, not noble, although she behaves as if she's the local laird's wife."

"Well, there's a start," enthused Rula. "That box of your mother's things, the ones I used for disguise, you have kept them long time, no? So have you other treasures, belonging to your father, perhaps? Something, some document with her name?"

It was true. After discovering all that cash, I'd been a bit distracted, and never quite finished clearing out the loft. My father had been meticulous in his record-keeping, maybe there were more secrets to discover. He'd never embraced the digital revolution and most everything he did to transact his business was on paper. I remembered how on a Sunday he'd be closeted away 'doing his books', as my mother used to complain.

After we'd showered and dressed, I went to fetch the ladder from the garage. Rula insisted she would accompany me into the loft. "We go up together," she insisted, "look for evidence of this Frenchwoman. Exciting, no?"

"No," I replied, "you stay here and I'll pass things down to you." I was behaving just like my father. I could imagine Rula putting her pretty feet though my bedroom ceiling. "And she's not French, by the way, not with a voice like that. Although there is likely a family connection way back."

Anyway, up there behind the cold water tank was a stack of small wooden boxes and several drawers from a card filing system. It took me an hour to manoeuvre them all over the rafters to the loft hatch; they were damned heavy, some of them, and I was balancing gingerly on narrow beams. Rula took them down, one by one, and laid them out in the spare bedroom, where I joined her with muted anticipation. I wasn't expecting this search to be fruitful, my dad never having ever referred to Mrs Delacroix other than to scorn the way she failed to use the land next her house for agriculture or development. He couldn't bear to see a resource go wasting.

The card file drawers were indeed just that, every one with a year printed on the front with a marker pen. They each contained hundreds of five by threes, all handwritten with names and dates in my father's recognisable hand, separated by dividers and grouped together by month. The names were occasionally quite exotic, mainly women's monikers like Glad Rose, Silke and Early Dawn, whilst others expressed emotions of robustness, such as Endurance, or suggested mysterious notions such as Deep Sound. This was all handwritten, as I said, in black ink. Most had times inked in, using the twenty-four hour clock, but some were instead struck through with a red line and the words scribbled against them, also in red, noting Storm, Alert, Tide or, most uncharacteristically for my father, Fuck-up.

None of the names on the cards was Delacroix, although whether the Duchess was a Rose or any of the other several dozen women's names I couldn't know. Nonetheless we persevered and looked though all the card file drawers. In addition to the names, the reverse of each card gave more information in what looked to be some kind of code, the letter B or M or W, for example, every one accompanied by a number qualified by what I assumed was a measurement and adding another name. So we would see, for instance 'T 20kg

Maurice'. In most cases, particularly on the more recent cards, these names were abbreviated to the initial capital.

So we turned to the small wooden boxes, which at first seemed randomly stuffed with papers of all shapes and sizes. They were held together in bunches by bulldog clips, again grouped by year and month. I quickly recognised some of them as invoices and others as receipts. All the invoices had been stamped 'PAID' with a date written across them in red ink. They were such a mixture I set them aside to peruse later, except for one invoice that caught my eye because of the sum that had been paid. It was from a civil engineer, which included separate fees from a structural engineer and an architect. No details were provided except for a reference to 'as per our agreed discussions and design proposal no. 76394/Min, dated May 1985'. Like I said, it was the sum paid that intrigued me: £347,000. I put the large, printed sheet on top of the pile, intending to examine it further, but there was more to see for now.

For we had also unearthed a collection of financial accounts with Benny's signature at the bottom—Bernardo, his full name because it was business. Income and outgoings all laid bare for the last twenty plus years before the old man kicked the bucket in a delirium of copulation. And here, here at last, there was precisely what we were looking for, entries both outgoing and incoming, many of them significantly large sums, Benny's typing overwritten in pen on several transactions with the name Delacroix.

"You see!" Rula was beside herself with glee. "Regular business associates. Rula has a nose for such things." Well, so now I had her nose to add to her other remarkable attributes. But yes, this was indeed a find.

The contents of the last box were more curious still. It was a collection of cuttings from newspapers, mainly the local or national Scottish newspapers. Some were very yellowed and it didn't need me to look for a date to know they were old. Most of these were articles about the history of Beachborough and its environs. Stuff I had read before, how in the eighteenth century our sleepy village had been a major sea port serving tea clippers and coal barges that sailed up along the east coast of Britain. There was even an item reporting the last ever consignment of coal being offloaded in the mid-twentieth century, with an opinion offered that the port would now decline, the estuary already silting up and without dredging considered to be useful only for leisure activities. I remembered how a windsurfing business started up around that time, or maybe it was a little later. One rather fictionalised tale told of smugglers coming up the river to the quay in days of yore, with mention of secret tunnels to the grand houses built by clipper captains, although these were pooh-poohed as local mythology on account of the coast being sandy and impossible to tunnel. It struck me that this was an over-cynical judgement given the large rabbit warrens and foxes dens I'd seen robustly constructed in the dunes. The largest collection of articles, however, consisted of factual reports: shipwrecks, storm warnings and the campaigns of Customs and Excise to maintain their punitive control of coastal business.

But where did all this leave us? It was very intriguing, but I prefer secrets when they become transparent. Light began to dawn on me when Rula gave a cry and flapped a sheet of newsprint in front of me. "Look, look," she pleaded, smoothing the wrinkled sheet on the bed top. 'Montrose Lass lost in haar' said the headline, giving a brief explanation of the tragedy that had occurred south of Aberdeen, at a date not too many years behind us.

"OK," I answered, not terribly excited, "so what? Surely you didn't know the girl."

"It's a boat, dummy, not a person. Found broken on the rocks, it says. Look, you have name and date. I have hunch. Look in cards."

A whore doesn't have to be a dimwit and I was impressed, for there, in the wad of index cards corresponding to the year and month of the Montrose Lass's demise, I found a card with the name Montrose Lass, the words struck through in red and a scribbled Fog and Wreck added. The reverse showed 'C 20 tonne McNab'.

"Good on you, inspired." I hugged Rula although I remained unsure how much further this discovery had taken us.

Yet our journey of detection didn't end there, for at the bottom of the box, beneath the last wad of invoices, my fingers found a packet, an empty cardboard condom packet. That is, when I say empty I mean there were none left of the dozen foil-wrapped prophylactics that once had been lodged there waiting for action; but what I did find inside was one of those small sealable plastic pouches that are used fairly ubiquitously in the DIY trade to hold screws and small fittings. Now, this was not empty but contained a key, a key that was attached to a blue metal fob imprinted with the logo of the Bank of Scotland. A grubby brown ticket with a seven digit number written upon it was also attached, together with the name Delacroix.

"Now we're getting somewhere," I exhaled, with some relief I might tell you. I'd feared Rula would want to go through all the newspaper cuttings, trying to match each story with an index card, which was too onerous a task for me just then.

"So," I began, stuffing the papers back in their boxes, "we have a definite connection between my father and Mrs Delacroix, although how strong a connection, it is not yet possible to confirm."

"Perhaps they were fucking," suggested Rula, and when I scoffed she said I was not of a worldly mien. "Look," she said, "they have several business transactions and he have her key. He come and go as he please. Don't you know all relationships between man and woman are, sooner or later, sexual."

But the key, I pointed out, did not look like a house key, and she should draw no conclusions from it having been kept in an empty condom packet. It was no ordinary-looking key and, although I'd never had one, with the Bank of Scotland mark and the numbered tag I was pretty sure it was the key to a safe deposit box.

There was only one Bank of Scotland branch left open in Aberdeen, the others having been 'rationalised' after business was lost to online banking, and I determined to pay a visit with my key. I already thought of it as mine, but for all I knew it might belong to the Duchess, and thus her presence could be required for the box to be accessed. That thought troubled me for several days before I plucked up enough courage to visit the bank.

When I explained my intention to Rula, she seemed rather exercised and warned me not to go wearing my long black leather coat and shades. "You know what nasty Frenchwoman say, you look like spy. Could be gangster too."

"Not French. I already told you. And do you think I'm daft enough to do that?" I did, however, resolve to leave my gun in the car. It's a while since I visited a bank and I had no idea whether a security system there might identify a lethal lump of metal in my pocket. "I'll wear a suit," I told her, "and carry a briefcase." That pacified her and we retired to my bedroom to celebrate having unravelled at least part of the mystery.

4

There was a beggar sitting each side of the front door to the bank. The first had a cardboard notice propped up against the wall stating that he was ex-army, had PTSD and was hungry. The second was a young woman with a scabby face who asked if I had any change for a coffee. I had no change, which I told her, none at all, and she hunched and pulled a face. Taking out my rather swollen wallet I handed her a fifty pound note, one of several I'd taken from the loft hoard for casual disposal. She looked surprised and rather irritated, so I bent to take it back, at which the ex-soldier gasped, "Give it 'ere, guv'nor, the slag don't deserve it, fucking junkie." Of course, sharing my father's view of the military I did no such thing, but swept past into the bank.

Inside the bank I was confronted by an unfamiliar environment. Gone was the traditional counter with cashiers sat behind a glass screen, having been replaced by four circular tables at which brightly-demeanour-ed young people sat in easy chairs in front of open laptops. There was no obvious place to queue, but as I stood wondering what to do next, a girl with an American smile called me over with promises to help me. She looked to be barely out of school and wore a badge with the slogan 'I'm Sam, your little helper'.

It turned out there were few formalities to prevent me from reaching safe deposit box 7539212, for that's what the key was intended for, as I had guessed. I had gone armed with my passport and my father's death certificate to prove I had a legitimate right to the box, but what really smoothed my path was the fact that I shared first names with my father who, it turned out, was the legitimate owner of the box. I had long been capable of reproducing his flamboyant signature, well proven on forged sick notes to school in my teens, and so was able to masquerade as him once more, awkwardly signing for his presence with a mouse in an electronic ledger on the girl's laptop. Thank goodness they haven't yet progressed to using electronic fingerprints, and how lucky I hadn't ever got round to closing his current account, was all I could think at that moment. For all the bank knew, my father was one of the new everlasting elderly. Anyway, it was a relief too to find I wasn't asked if I was Mr Delacroix.

The girl badged as Sam stood and shook hands, proposing to take me down to 'the vault', but as I rose from my chair she frowned, tut-tutted and muttered under her breath, "Just look at that. They have a cheek, don't they, benefit scum." She was glancing across at the next table, where the young woman beggar with a scabby face, who had tidied her hair and crudely applied some lipstick, was attempting to convert her fifty pounds windfall into smaller denominations. The teller, a young man who was looking harassed, was explaining that the note was no good and he demanded to know where she had found it. When she kept silent, he waved over a large man in a uniform, who I guessed was security. "Trying to pass a dud

52

note," I heard the young man say, at which I hurried after the American smile who was heading for some stairs down, set discreetly in the floor and identified only by a chrome guardrail.

The room containing the bank's safe deposit boxes was situated at the end of a short corridor in the basement, behind a metal door that the girl opened using a keypad. Behind the door was a kind of steel portcullis that rose into the ceiling once she entered another code on a second wall-mounted device. The room itself was a rather bleak affair, with numbered grey container fronts set into three walls from floor to ceiling. A table and chair was placed against the fourth wall.

The portcullis closed behind us, I noticed, and I remarked how it would be a problem if the electricity were to fail at this juncture. "It depends who you're stuck in here with," Sam answered, with a demonstrably louche leer, it seemed to me. I could have been tempted but I'm no cradle-snatcher, so I turned to the business of finding my box, which happened to be lodged right in front of me. What she was doing in here with me was a puzzle; from what I had seen in films I'd expected her to wait outside. This felt most irregular.

Of course, I had wondered what I would find in the box, my first thought being that it would be cash, possibly jewellery—although I had no more need of cash right then. But what was revealed, when the box was extracted from the wall and its lid opened, was a single folded piece of paper. I lifted the box onto the table and the girl said I could sit and examine the contents there if I wished. But, on second thoughts, I would have preferred more privacy, and I put the document inside my briefcase, replacing and locking the box in its cavity in the wall.

The girl was, meanwhile, looking agitated and I raised a questioning eyebrow.

"Shit!" she exclaimed, "they're always reminding us, stay outside the vault while a client conducts his business privately." There, I had been correct in my assumption. She shrugged and shook the portcullis: "Can't reach the fucking code plate, an' if I have to call emergency I'll be in for it." I remembered, the device she had used to open the portcullis was quite high on the wall. Had this all been a ruse? I have a suspicious mind and an unruly imagination.

Well, there was nothing else for it: "Could you activate the portcullis code kind of backwards, like if I lift you up high enough to reach?" She grinned and nodded.

So that's what I did, I grasped her at knee level and hoisted her as high as the top of the door opening. She was a slight thing and clung to me tightly, so it was not a difficult lift for a man who works out every day. With her arm through an opening, she was successful on her third attempt, and I pulled her back quickly when the portcullis began to roll upward, so that she wouldn't be jammed in the mechanism. We fell backwards onto the floor together, the first time I'd held a taut young teen in my arms for many years, but there was no way I was going to be netted by what was evidently a foxy creature. Like I said, banks are unrecognisable these days. You used to know where you were with brilliantined mature men wearing pinstripe suits.

As I exited the bank, relieved to be away from Sam's oppressive presence, as it seemed to me, I noticed the soldier had gone. The woman with the scabby face was back sitting cross-legged on her blanket and when she saw me she gave me the finger. Charity is such a thankless business.

It was three days since Rula and I had gone through the papers from the loft and I'd promised to tell her what I found in the safe deposit box, but I wanted to get home first, to take a closer look at the document I'd retrieved. I'd had enough of Rula reading her own meanings into matters of my family business.

Once home, I unfolded the paper carefully on the kitchen table. The heading at the top of the document immediately indicated that it was some kind of legal document, there was the name, address and telephone number of an Edinburgh notary, embossed with gold lettering. I won't reproduce the whole content here, you might be some kind of identity vulture with a digitizer, photoshopping software and printer, and you're not going to misappropriate my treasure trove. But I can tell you the gist of it all, which fairly struck me dumb, or would have done if there was someone else present at the time, other than Sniffer, who'd find me temporarily unable to communicate. It read like the codicil to a will, signed *E Delacroix* and witnessed, and it was headed 'Knock Hall, Disposition and Entitlements', going on to explain that upon the death of the owner of said house and associated lands, Mrs Evangeline Delacroix, she being without issue, ownership would pass to…and here was my astonishment, for the name and address of the beneficiary was none other than that of my father. Even more attention grabbing, in the event that his death preceded that of the current owner, Mrs Delacroix, title of both house and lands would pass to his elder son. Me of all people. There were further caveats and qualifications saying what would happen if I too were dead, my brother being named as the next in line, but I didn't really pay much attention to these, for I was in good health and keen to think of myself as the owner of a tasty little estate overlooking an unspoilt nature reserve.

Well, you can imagine, I was completely discombobulated by this discovery. I mean, I lead a fairly humble life; with the money from the loft cleaned I had already been looking forward to a comfortable existence, but I have never aspired to owning extravagant property. Conspicuous wealth was just not my thing. With that thought in mind, for the immediate moment I completely forgot to question how this inheritance had come about in the first place. My stupor did not last.

I made a couple of copies of the document on my printer-copier, marked them as COPY, and filed the original with my own private papers. Having satisfied myself that it was securely hidden from the world I went and sat with a brandy to calm my excitement. That's when all the questions started bubbling up like gas in a geyser. As I have already mentioned, my father had only referred to the owner of Knock Hall in fairly negative terms, so how was it that she was going to give everything away to him, now me? I began to imagine confronting her with the document and hearing her tell me to 'sling your hook, peasant'. I remembered what Rula had suggested, that the two of them had been fuck-buddies and, thinking of Rula, I was overcome with the urge to share my information with someone I trusted. In hindsight, maybe that someone would have best been Benny, since his trusted business dealings with my father might have included knowledge of the Delacroix woman, but it was Rula whom I

56

telephoned. I suppose I had grown quite close to her over the past week or so.

She was between jobs and said she'd be over, and it was only twenty minutes later her bright blue Porsche Boxster was shining incongruously in my mossy driveway at the side of the house. "I cannot stay long," she said, "I have special client in an hour."

"Wowsers!" she hooted, when I showed her a copy of the legal document (I don't know where she had heard it but it has become an oft-repeated word in her adopted vocabulary). "Wowsers! This some surprise come-out." She gave me a quick hug. "You rich man now. I told Frenchwoman had connection."

"She's not…" oh why bother. "Well, not quite a rich man yet." (I was forgetting the hoard from my loft.) "There's many a slip, and I might find she's made a subsequent change to her declared intentions."

Rula was not interested in my caution, she was reading the document closely, her eye following her index finger as it traced down the page. I assumed it was just her fascination in reading legal English. Then her head bobbed up. "What this?" she asked, pointing. "I not know this. What is saltire?"

I was surprised she hadn't yet come across the term for the Scottish flag, and I explained what it was and what it looked like.

"Hmph!" she scoffed. "Why would crazy Frenchwoman leave everything to flag?"

I took the sheet of paper from her whilst she kept pointing. There, at the bottom of the list of reserve beneficiaries, two names after my brother, which I had not troubled to read, thinking the arrangements all rather excessive, was the last entry. In black and white it decreed that if everyone else in the cascade above was deceased at the time of Mrs Delacroix's passing, the house and estate was to be given over to a beneficiary named as the Saltire, North East Chapter. Not a flag but, going by there being an address, what looked to be an organisation. I had never heard of it.

I stood puzzling whether this mattered anyway, since I was alive and hoped to be for many years yet, when Rula jumped up and declared she had to leave.

"I have special client. Big Mac. He bring two sons for sixteenth birthday treat. You know what happen if I not be there and ready."

Big Mac and his brother Ronnie were probably the city's most notorious thugs, and Mac's twin boys were equally well known on account of them terrorising the other kids at their school, reports of their violence and extortion having reached the local daily press on several occasions. I felt concerned for Rula's wellbeing, but she said she had done business with Big Mac before and he had behaved himself, if roughly. Furthermore, Benny would be in the building, so she was not going to be completely on her own. She promised to call me later, and I gave her a large brown envelope to pass to Benny. It contained £25,000 in used fifty pound notes, the latest batch to be cleaned.

I was sharing my four cheese pizza with Sniffer around seven o'clock when she rang. It wasn't the usual self-confident Rula, her voice was full of cracks. "How'd it go?" I ventured to ask, fully expecting she'd had a tough session with the McAllisters.

"Go on, he won't bite you, Daisy," I heard Magda's voice in the background, using Rula's professional cover name and encouraging her. There was a long intake of breath, then Rula came back more smoothly: "Well, the first one was very excited. He was no problem, all over in a matter of seconds. But the other lad, my goodness, he wanted nothing of it. He could not be persuaded; he wasn't going to have his privates go anywhere near a slag like me—Big Mac came in from the other room and cuffed him for that—and he slouched off into the corner. I went over to him but when I touched his arm he shivered and slipped out through the bedroom door. I believe he might be homosexual from the bitch faces he pulls. I heard him moving about whilst I put on some clothes but when I went out into the living room to explain things to Big Mac, who'd gone there for a smoke, I found all three had left, and all I saw through the open door was a rear view of the gay son hastening along the landing."

"So, no violence or anything nasty?" I was certainly relieved—and amused. Fancy Big Mac, Aberdeen's self-styled tough guy, having a shirt-lifter for a son. Useful information.

She came back after a moment of silence. "No, no violence, but…but…"

"Yes?"

She continued in a rush: "You know that package you asked me to deliver to Benny?"

I was suddenly feeling too sick to answer.

"Well, I was late back, they were already here, waiting, so I quickly stuffed it inside Magda's flight case, behind the sofa, so it was out of view. But later, when I heard Benny talking on the landing, I went to get it, but…I'm really sorry…but…"

"It was no longer there. Yes, I get it. Rula, I already guessed. Fucking criminals."

Relatively, it was not a huge amount of money, just a minor portion from my huge hoard. It was the fact that this big fat scumbag, or maybe one of his scummy progeny, had abused Rula's hospitality, that's what did it for me. I tried to calm her down, not an easy thing over the phone. I could hear Magda offering her a glass of palinka and knew that at least I wouldn't be seeing the Porsche arriving this evening. Rula is easily tipsy, especially on Romanian plum brandy, so I wouldn't have her crying on my shoulder.

But as for McAllister, he wasn't someone I might approach and demand the return of my money. I thought of my gun but some good soul up in heaven got into my head and persuaded me it was not a good idea. The bullet would probably end up in me in any confrontation with that family.

"Put it down to experience," I urged Rula. "And tell Benny the McAllisters are banned from our businesses. I'll come see you in a day or two."

"Already done," she slurred. The change in her voice made me realise how much better had been her grasp of English grammar while she was under stress. Paradoxical.

It was only a week later I was able to enjoy a little schadenfreude after this most unfortunate event. I was in at Kwik-Fit, getting two new tyres fitted, and somebody had left a copy of the Evening Express newspaper. The oblique front page headline was typical of that rag: 'North East Man in Counterfeiting Inquiry'. The report went on to explain that police were investigating the several hospitality businesses of local man Bobby 'Big Mac' McAllister, 42, in connection with the recovery of a large sum of counterfeit banknotes. Suspicion had been aroused when a son of McAllister had attempted to purchase a top of the range electric guitar from the Slick Riffs music shop in King Street, paying cash with a wad of fifty pound notes and raising the wariness of the sales staff. No one had yet been charged but police confirmed that a quantity of class A drugs had been discovered in the store room of the Purple Rooster, one of McAllister's dance clubs. Mr McAllister is currently being held on suspicion, pending...et cetera et cetera. The story put me in such a good mood I gave the tyre fitter a twenty pound tip (using cash I knew for certain was genuine. I'm no fool).

But this counterfeiting angle worried me. Was all of the money from the loft fake? Because if it was, our laundering operation was simply courting danger, and had already been for quite some time. Had we really been cleaning what was essentially Monopoly money? The answer to that question came from an unexpected quarter.

5

Actually, I still had that other question to put to bed, although it was not something to keep me awake at night, just a bit of curiosity. But who were the Saltire, or to be more precise, the North East Chapter of the Saltire? A bit of Googling was all that was needed to provide an answer, and I printed what I found in order to show Rula. According to several articles it turned out that the Saltire is, according to which flavour of newspaper you read, either a philanthropic charity with an interest in supporting the development of health and wellbeing of young Scots men, or a political organisation with a fundamentally radical agenda. Despite having its roots in the now defunct SNLA, who were sometimes dubbed the tartan terrorists, and whilst its underlying ambition is independence for Scotland, the Saltire is not an assembly of violent activists and saboteurs. Instead, it has been variously described by the media of all persuasions as a respectable if eccentric pressure group engaged in exposing and pursuing the iniquities that it considers are visited upon Scotland by being in the union with England. I found a link to its web page, where its office bearers and board membership were given openly under its 'who we are' tab, its executive and non-executive directors but not its chairman or patron, the list seeming to comprise a range of respected business names, academics and a sprinkling of gentry. As for the North East Chapter, it seems the whole of Scotland had been carved up into manageable unitary divisions, which each have been given the oddly reverent name of chapter.

So, fine, I now had an idea what they were, but why they should be the potential beneficiaries of an elderly woman living quietly here in Beachborough, and beneficiaries in contention with my father at that, remained a puzzle. It added further mystery to my deceased old man's activities. Had he been involved with the Saltire, I wondered. Moving to Scotland had certainly changed his perspective on British politics, and he'd always voted for the SNP once he had formed a view about government from London. That was no secret. But there had been no evidence of him being an active member of any independence-minded group, other than the one time he'd attended a local SNP Burns night dinner hosted by our MP, Alex Salmond. Hardly incriminating, I'd say, he simply knew the man to be an entertaining speaker.

There was only one way to resolve the clutch of questions that were buzzing in my head. I had to go see Mrs Delacroix. I also resolved to take Benny with me, he's far more affable than me, he can be cringeworthily polite in a continental sort of way and he always dresses smart—not Italian dapper but soberly business-like. I hoped he might charm her.

But I have to digress a little at the moment, and I promise it's apposite. The thing is, I'm sure you've had plenty of those experiences when you've been thinking of something or someone and then, out of the blue that something or someone turns up wholly unexpectedly at your door. Usually totally unrelated to the present circumstances of your life's routine.

63

It's not what I'd call coincidence but something rather more spooky, as if one had been given a dog's uncanny sense of prescience. Well, whatever, that's what happened to me the morning after I did my little piece of research on the Saltire organisation.

I had printed out some of the information from their web site so that I might show Benny, thinking he may have heard of them on account of the wide circles in which he mixes, and I was reading it through over a coffee and toast when there came a knock at the front door. '*Oh no,*' I thought, '*that'll be Rula come to wring her very emotional European hands over the loss of my money.*' But instead, upon opening the door, I was confronted by a man with an unmistakably military bearing, in probably his mid to late fifties. He wore a plaid cap, cloak, stout boots and cavalry twills, and seemed in all as if he was dressed for a shoot. I immediately started asking myself what I might have done to upset the local landowning community. Was this a consequence of Sniffer's pheasant hunting exploits, for instance?

But no, he was very polite from the outset, smiling and asking in a very brisk tone had he the pleasure of speaking to the home owner, at which of course I had no reason to dissemble. "Well, good," he answered cheerily, "I am Major Frisk." He then stopped and stared me in the face, expectantly. Was I supposed to know this Major Frisk, 'cos I didn't. He too looked puzzled by my silence. The penny then dropped. As I have previously intimated, I had not made a big noise about my father's demise; carelessly, I hadn't even advised the bank, as I have told you, or put an In Memoriam in the local newspaper. So it was probable this Major Frisk had come expecting to find my father, although it was obvious they'd never met, since although I shared his name I didn't look anything like a man in his eighties.

I decided to play along with him, he didn't seem threatening. "How may I help you, sir?" I asked. "Would you like to come in?" After a routine bout of barking, reserved for unknown visitors, Sniffer had pushed his way to the fore and was examining the man's trouser-legs, his tail waving his usual flag of friendly intent.

Major Frisk looked down and bent to stroke Sniffer's ears. "No, I won't trouble you like that, thank you all the same," he replied, in clipped English speech devoid of any Scottish accent. "It's just I was in the area and thought I'd make one of our periodic calls. I noticed yesterday that it's been a couple of years at least, very remiss indeed, but..." he looked away, appearing to be concentrating on something far away up the hill, then remarked, "but of course, old Walter passed away and the silly girl in the office hasn't kept matters up to date. That's what's happened, yes. No continuity, you see, ten pence short of a shilling that girl. Anyway," he seemed to be mentally hoisting up his bootlaces, "anyway, so here I am, come to call. Bridging a gap, so to speak."

I looked at him, trying to look inquisitive without appearing impudent. "And...?" I prompted, although clearly I should have known why he'd come. Mentioning the name Walter would have been the deliberate confirmation as to his credentials.

He bent his face close to mine. "It is still safe, I assume," he almost whispered. "The merchandise. No-one, er, no pesky hounds come sniffing around?"

"Only Sniffer here," I answered with a laugh, patting my dog on the head.

65

"All fine and dandy, then," he smiled. "Only we do worry. It is important to check, not that we don't trust you. The Saltire cares deeply about its custodians. You know that of course."

And their money, obviously.

He eyeballed me, long and hard. "I suppose it's very much like looking after radioactive waste," he finally asserted. What a bizarre thing for him to say. "Hot and dangerous if allowed to leak out," he concluded. "Wouldn't you say so?"

"But we have it well contained," I answered, not knowing what the fuck he was talking about but picking what I thought was an appropriate response to his metaphor.

"Hmm," his face creased into a sinuous grin. "Very well, I have no need to take a look, of course. Did Walter always do that, make a physical check, here and, er, up the road? Well, never mind that now. I'm sorry to have interrupted your day. The Saltire will be in touch very soon, usual place, to advise your replacement liaison. Our omission, I must admit. But poor Walter, the price of chasing Bacchus I'm afraid. Ah well, tootle-pip, nice to meet you." And he was away, his country boots marching to the rhythm of a military pattern he'd begun to hum.

Of course I was suspicious. This man had made a point of coming to assure himself—or assure his organisation—that something valuable my father was looking after for him was still secure. But he'd not wanted to check for himself, just take my (or rather, as far as he was aware, my father's word) that everything was 'fine and dandy'. After my experience with the dognapper, I had been wondering if the whole episode had been a cover for something more sinister than a cloak and dagger conversation on my sunny front step. Had this been a recce?

But I'm not thick and immediately I began to join up the dots. Saltire and money were both very current terms in my consciousness; so that was one connection sorted. That the money might be hot I had already considered, especially after the incidents with the beggar at the bank and the Big Mac affair. But the matter of my father being a custodian of it for someone else, now that was a real mystery. Perhaps Mrs Delacroix was going to be able to shed a lot more light on this entire conundrum than I had meant initially to question her about.

Benny agreed to come with me the next afternoon. We had lunch together first, and I filled him in as much as I could, including warning him about the counterfeit angle.

"The money, it is good," he assured me. "That is, the English notes. I check it all before moving it on." He shook his head with a grimace. "Some banknotes issued by the two Scottish banks, however, they are not so good, no longer valid, I knew because they are paper, but so far there have been very few of these you have passed to me."

I decided to examine the hoard before we went out. I had a definite hunch. The money I'd given to Rula for Benny and which Big Mac or his son had stolen, much to their ruin, I remember taking from the smallest suitcase. I'd been in a hurry: Rula was on her way over and I wanted to have it packaged ready for her, so I'd grabbed the smallest and lightest case simply because it was easiest, and extracted several bundles of notes. I went up there now and opened that same case. All the notes it contained were of Scottish issue. I tumbled the tied bundles and found not a single English note.

67

I then opened the two other cases and, as I had begun to expect, their contents were exclusively English banknotes. The contents of both of these two cases was seriously depleted, whilst the third case seemed relatively more full. What I'd done was obvious; almost exclusively, I'd been feeding Benny notes from the two larger cases. I can't explain why. Perhaps I was just nervous, wanting to shift the largest bulk of my hoard before something went wrong. Who knows, but here was some kind of answer: the saltire sticker on the front of the smallest suitcase, it wasn't there as a souvenir of some adventure in the highlands, it signified ownership. The Saltire organisation. Bits of what had happened now made some kind of sense, although the situation as a whole lacked reason. In particular, why the money was stored here in my loft I could not explain.

At least, I could reassure Benny that he'd not been handling much in the way of counterfeit or obsolete banknotes, at which he grinned and, with a tap of his finger against his nose, confided that he knew how to handle such a challenge. So it was that we set off in a cheery mood to make our call at Knock Hall. Despite my dislike of traffic disturbing the rural quiet of Knockhall Road, I agreed that Benny would drive us there. He had a brand new Jaguar I-PACE, which I'd forgotten but which I hoped would help reassure Mrs Delacroix that we were no mere pair of toe-rags come to size up what pickings there might be had from her property.

She came to the door dressed entirely in black leather, which startled me and clearly amused Benny. "I didn't expect a geriatric dominatrix," he told me later. She uttered not a word of greeting but simply stood in the open porch doorway and stared imperiously at us both in turn.

"Good morning," I ventured, but that's as far as I got.

"And what is good about it, that you have come to my house?" she snapped. "I thought our business at the crossroads was concluded, is that not so?"

A picture is worth a thousand words, or so they say. I didn't have a picture but in my coat pocket was one of the facsimiles of the legal document from the safe deposit box. So that was my answer and I unfolded it, holding it up for her to read.

Taking the document, she was silent for a while, then in a quieter tone, "How long? For some time I've presumed he'd gone. But how long now since he passed?"

"A little more than two years last Christmas."

"So I assume you know everything," she declared.

"Not quite," I had to admit.

"Which is why you are here," she explained to herself. I couldn't make out whether she was regretting our appearance at her door.

"Well, I suppose you had better come in," she sighed, "and your spruce little friend. Bum chums, are you?"

It was not the impression I had intended to give and I was taken aback by her offensive frankness.

"Bernardo, here, was my father's trusted accountant." My introduction of Benny simply resulted in a raised eyebrow, but she let us both over the threshold.

She ushered us into a room lined with books, with a wide bay window that looked out towards the distant dunes of the nature reserve. The air in the house was cold and everything had that smell of oldness that one always finds in centuries-old properties which have long stood unmodernised, while the world around them has moved forward.

"You are the elder son, I take it," she asserted, "and your father told you nothing about our business I am certain. Never a better example of discretion than your father."

She sat back in an uncomfortable-looking wooden chair at the table that was set in front of the empty fireplace, carefully studying the disposition document through a pair of wire-framed spectacles. In her shiny leather, I fancied she was some kind of sprite or demon, something that had come down the chimney or up through the bare floorboards. Out of her dungarees and wellington boots she was certainly no country duchess.

It wasn't only the air that was cool, there was an icy chill filling the space between us, which her studied look of irritated disinterest was feeding with spiky glances. The warm spark of motivation that had brought me here had extinguished and, mentally shivering, I struggled to find words to engage her in conversation. The words I eventually chose were foolish as an opener and as soon as I spoke them I couldn't understand why I had picked this topic as an introduction. It must simply have been festering at the back of my mind.

"I don't wish to pry," I started, "but were you and my father...?"

"Don't be pathetic!" she retorted, biting off my sentence. "I know that's all you people think about these days, but no, we were not lovers, although I'm sure I did love the man."

Well, that was me firmly put in my place.

Then she was on her feet, moving with the spring of a much younger woman. "Come on," she commanded, throwing down the document and her spectacles. "I know why you have come. Come with me and I'll show you what you desire to see. Bring your companion if you wish." She pulled a face as she said that and I made a mental note to firmly disabuse her about Benny's sexuality.

She led us down a long dreary hallway, past two or three firmly closed dark wooden doors, at last unlocking and easing open the apparently heavy door that brought the hallway to an end. Abruptly, as we stepped forward to pass through, she stopped us with an arm across the space and stood examining us from head to toe. "I'm dressed for this," she asserted, "and you'll probably do," directed at me, "but your friend might well spoil his pretty suit." She opened a trunk that stood just inside the door and retrieved two long gabardine raincoats. "Put these on," she directed, "both of you. It can get very mucky down there. Not as effective as leather but it'll save your clothes from permanent staining. I can't do anything about your shoes."

As I removed my own coat she saw me transfer my gun to a pocket in the gabardine.

"You won't need that here," she snapped. "No-one has ever managed to find their way into this place. Not since..." And with that breath of inconclusion we were pushed through the doorway, hearing her lock and bolt the door behind us.

Almost immediately, steps went down, stone steps made from natural rock, and I realised we had entered some kind of tunnel with an arched roof and correspondingly curved walls. It made me think of the entrance to a London underground station. As we progressed, lights came on overhead, in response to some hidden motion sensor. I counted thirty steps, this passage was going deeper than a traditional basement. Our shoes were loud on the stone but with no echo, and as the lights came on I observed that the wooden panelling which had covered the walls had now been replaced by reinforced concrete. It was clearly damp down here, the wire in the concrete was rusty and it was possible to make out the shape of the mesh. Brushing against the wall I found my raincoat quickly smeared with a damp brown residue that quickly crystallised.

"Don't try it for yourself," said Mrs Delacroix, noticing, "but that is salt. Amongst other things left from the blasting."

Suddenly the steps came to an end and we were standing in the quiet of a sandy floor. The passage ahead continued its downward path, but not steeply, and I could see that just ahead it curved to the right. Once beyond the bend the condition of the walls and ceiling began to deteriorate. There were cracks and fissures, through which fine sand trickled as we passed. Floor and ceiling too were beginning to come closer together and I found I was stooping.

Around the next bend, a slight left this time, conditions quickly worsened, and our host bade us stop while she removed a large flashlight from its bracket. In the light from the torch, we could see some distance further down the passage, beyond where the overhead lights were lit, to where part of the roof appeared to have collapsed and there was a major ingress of sand heaped across the floor. I could hear the tinkle of water dripping in the farthest distance.

"They told us this would last a hundred years," she grumbled. "Cost a pretty penny too. But the engineers never explained about maintenance." She brought the light back along the wall. "Still, it's all here, untouched, and safe for the moment." She raked the light over a long column of black coffers that had been set along the wall, each one more than a metre in length and bound with metal straps. They looked like the sort of thing one imagines having carried pirate booty in centuries past. Only these belonged to more recent times, with combination locks securing their lids.

"Listen to me," Mrs Delacroix commanded rather than invited. "What is in these cases is not mine, nor was it the property of your father. No, we were the unwilling guardians. What remains of ours lies further down there, beyond the roof fall. But I leave the matter of its recovery to you, since it is rightfully yours. Also yours, once I am gone, is the responsibility to safeguard what is held here. She deftly opened a lock and pulled up a coffer lid. The underside of the lid was insulated against dampness by a tarry looking liner, as was the inside of the coffer itself."

The first thing we saw in the opened coffer was a large blue and white cloth, a saltire flag I realised, folded over what lay inside. Beneath, under several layers of heavily waxed material, were wrapped the intimidating shapes of automatic weapons, cold, black and lifeless like dread skeletons in their coffins, waiting silently to be brought to deadly life.

Benny, who hadn't spoken, reached in and pulled out a gun. "Mama mia," he whistled, "I thought these were toys at first but, no, this is the real business." He held the gun at his hip and pretended to spray bullets into the darkness. "Look," he said, pointing at a maker's marque, "made in Czechoslovakia. Since when have we been importing Soviet weapons?"

"It's Czech Republic, Benny. A democracy these days."

"Not then, it wasn't, when your old man was in business. Well, only the latter stages. That all happened in 1993, he wasn't retired yet. I reckon someone was offloading this stuff once the place became independent."

73

"Please stop," insisted Mrs Delacroix, taking the weapon and returning it to the case. "I hope never to see these taken out and used in earnest."

I looked at her quizzically. "By whom?" was my obvious question.

She looked at me with a mixture of surprise and disbelief. "You've had a visit, of course." She gave a humourless grin. "From the Saltire, I mean."

She locked the coffer lid and beckoned for us to follow her back the way we had come. "I'll make coffee," she said, her air of mystery temporarily dispelled by the words. "You will be expecting an explanation."

"It has been quite a number of years since we ceased trading." She dropped liquid from a pipette into her coffee cup, without further elucidation, and took a small sip with a sigh. "But back then the tunnel was already proving difficult, and the estuary was silting up. Then there was the business with Saltire—that put the proverbial lid on everything. '*Well, we'd made our fortunes, or so,*' we thought, '*it seemed the appropriate time to pack it all in.*' Neither of us wanted any involvement with terrorism. Sadly, we agreed that the two of us must sever all connection, everything would have to go dark for a goodly while. As for separating our complex business entanglement, you have in your possession the document that was our solution. A similar one was drawn up to provide for me and my descendants, but then I have no issue, so it was irrelevant. I destroyed it almost immediately. Your father was the brains of our business, I did not resent him having the lion's share. He'd made a far greater investment in more ways than one."

"So," I ventured, "you were gunrunners?"

She fixed me with a cold stare.

"Did you not know your father? Gunrunners indeed. No, that's Saltire business, not ours. No, we were importers. Adventurer importers I called us. Superior cloths, fine wines, rare spices—all the kind of special things that make the material life a pleasant experience, and the excise man wants to preserve for only the wealthy to enjoy. The occasional narcotics too, I have to admit, not huge quantities. I've always approved of the individual's right to choose his mode of destruction so long as it does not interfere with another's."

She saw the look on my face.

"What on earth were you thinking all that time as you grew up? Where did you think the money came from that brought you good food and a childhood free from want?" Her expression was one of astonishment edged with scorn. She downed the last of her coffee.

"I suppose we were lucky that the Saltire got wind of our little enterprise so late on. As I said, we'd made our fortunes, well, enough to be comfortable at least, and were able to secrete most of our cash away before they began to take an interest. But of course we were operating beyond the law, and they had that on us. There was nothing we could do to prevent them from moving in, using our passageway for storage. The guns you have seen, whilst their store of funny money had to be removed and dispersed when it was threatened with becoming obsolete. You know about the transition to polymer notes, of course."

I grimaced, which she saw, and she laughed wryly, a sharp cry like a vixen.

"Blackmailed!" she exclaimed. "That had always been the risk we ran, always dealing with a number of dodgy characters as we did. But those people, the merchants and the seamen they engaged, they always stood to lose, for our business was very good business for a number of independent entrepreneurs, and they wouldn't have wanted it to go down. Yet here at last we were being blackmailed, and I was far more nervous seeing them unload the guns from boats than I'd ever been with our own merchandise coming ashore. And we couldn't stop them."

"I felt it was divine intervention when the tunnel roof collapsed at the river end. But they'd already brought in a lot of stuff. Enough for a small army. I still read the newspapers avidly, waiting to hear of impending insurrection, but so far there are only hints and rumours. They come here periodically, less frequently of late, just to check that everything is secure, but with never a word about their plans."

She poured herself another coffee from the silver percolator and walked with it to the window. Her words became soft and trancelike as she spoke to the world outside.

"I suppose now he's gone I have only myself to protect." Then she stood erect, struck by a thought. *'What is the expression you people use?'* She turned on her heel. *'Blow the gaff, isn't that it? I could, I suppose, turn the lot of them in, probably be rewarded for it.'*

"But..."

"There's no need for you to worry," she snapped. "The money is safe; I assume you've found it. Only this little piece of paper connects us." She picked up the copy of the Knock Hall disposition from the table where she had left it under her spectacles. "Well, I'm not dead yet, so this for you remains a gift in waiting. No-one knew about it except the signature witness, and he lies six feet under that aspen on the far side of my lawn. Natural causes," she added, seeing my startled look.

"But why is the Saltire included as a beneficiary if they have brought you such difficulties?" The more I'd listened the greater this had become a puzzle.

"My little revenge," she chuckled. "You being named as inheritor, the hoi polloi would likely dismiss you as my lovechild. But inheritance by The Saltire, well…Disposal of an estate like this in the suspicious world of politics would bring scrutiny, and scrutiny is what men of The Saltire do their best to avoid. You'd be okay were it all to come to you. You have no secret profile, nothing to hide as far as I am aware. Now," she said in an abruptly pointed conclusion, "there is nothing more I wish to say. You need not return. I mentioned there are some effects that belong to you at the tunnel far end, but they are not perishable, although I'm not sure they are even safely retrievable. You will have to wait until the estate is yours to find out. Meantime, I recommend that you keep your little gun close to hand, these people have no need to harm you but who knows what goes through minds like that."

She chivvied us to the front door, and I noticed her double barrelled shotgun slotted in the elephant's foot umbrella stand.

"Have a nice day," she cooed, her irony dripping like a burst spleen.

"That woman," said Benny, the car doors firmly closed, "her whole speech sounded like she was talking to herself. Like she was making it up as she went along. I'd say she was drunk."

"Doesn't get out much, that's all," I answered. "Mad as a hatter." But that was just me trying to mask my own confusion

77

over the veracity of the tale we'd been told. And if she was an alcoholic who'd be surprised, with her living all alone up there with that secret under her feet?

6

I must admit it had been an interesting encounter, but I could kick myself for allowing the woman to have shown us out before I'd asked the questions that were jostling in my head. It's always been like that with me, always thinking of the best retort long after the moment had passed, finding my own urgent questions had been deferred in the wake of what others had to say. My dad said, "I think too much," whereas clearly, he'd been a man of action.

But I certainly had plenty to think about the next morning when I went into town for my promised catch-up with Rula. Magda caught me at the top of the stairs, her face pale with woe.

"Please don't be angry with her," she blurted.

Well, I'd already decided the incident with the stolen banknotes should be put down to experience. No point blaming Rula. I said as much to Magda.

"No, no," she pleaded, "she'd never dealt with him before, she would have called Mr Benny, but…"

She could see I was not following this at all.

"Rula hurt. He beat her. You be kind."

She opened the door to their apartment to reveal Rula sitting on the couch, a spent cigarette in her mouth, one more

79

almost ready to join the heap of butts in the ashtray in front of her. She had her right arm in a sling and her left eye was black and closed.

"I'm sorry," she whispered. "He hurt me, I thought I might die. Only, Magda heard and saved me."

Her story drew pity from me, and also alarm. Despite being barred, Ronnie McAllister had visited Rula. I'd heard he looked nothing like his brother, Big Mac, for whilst both of them were built like a wrestler, Ronnie was said to be a man of modest height, and lacking Big Mac's huge Desperate Dan face. Big Mac dressed perennially in grubby sportswear but, reputedly, Ronnie had a penchant for fashionable haircuts and expensive suits. Tony on the front counter hadn't given him a second look and Rula had found his appearance over the video link to be quite engaging. Any resemblance to his bullish brother was not immediately obvious.

"So," she explained through her swollen lips, "we did the business and it all seemed very normal. Then without any hint that something was wrong, and whilst he was still inside me, he put his hands around my throat and squeezed really tight, saying 'you fucking bitch, now you're gonna tell me everything'. I had his full weight on top of me, he's a solid bastard, and his elbows were pinning down my shoulders. I was so scared, and confused, I could feel everything going faint."

I sensed my ire increasing as she spoke these words, and in a useless reflex I felt for the gun in my pocket.

"But what did he want from you?"

"He said he was here on behalf of his brother, who had been stitched up, and I was to tell him who'd done it. Done what, I croaked, and he then told me about the money and his

80

brother being Big Mac and everything. I wasn't saying nothing, so he reached over to the bottle of wine we'd half emptied as an introduction and poured the rest of it into my mouth until it overflowed. I was choking for real now. If I didn't tell him where the money came from, he said, he was going to shove the bottle up my private parts so I could never work again. At that, I must have blacked out."

This was horrifying. I sat and put my arm around her shoulder but she shook me off.

"No," she said, "you're going to be angry." She shifted away from me on the couch and took on a determined look. "When I came round," she continued, "I found he hadn't moved and, as soon as he saw my eyes opening, he tightened his fingers around my neck even more. I knew he was serious and the sight of that empty bottle sitting there made my blood run cold. So, I know you'll hate me for this, but I had to tell him everything. About your inheritance, the posh woman's estate and all of it. He wouldn't let go until I had said all of it. I was frightened for my life."

"She was frightened for her life," echoed Magda in support.

Rula's apparent defencelessness didn't match my understanding that she was practised in martial arts, but then I hadn't been there to see how she'd been restrained, and maybe her earlier claim of skills in self-defence had been mere bravado to win my admiration. I had a girlfriend once who, on learning of my particular love of dogs, wove a complex tale of her adventures with her own very graphically-described dog, now sadly deceased. I learned from her mother, years later, how she'd never owned a dog, or a cat, or even a goldfish. Such are the illustrious lies women weave to catch their lustful prey.

"So he knows about my stash." Considering the individual that Rula had described I had good reason to share her fears.

"Evil," said Rula and Magda, nodding ruefully together, and Rula went on: "Once I'd told him, I thought it was all over, but he didn't get up and go. I was still in dread of that bottle. Then he said he wasn't going to pay me for the session, but before he'd be on his way he was going to have his pleasure all over again. I just lay still in dread while he went about it, but when he'd finished, he said I had been a disappointing fuck and he was going to teach me a lesson. He…" Her lip trembled and she reached for another cigarette, which Magda had to light for her. "…he took the bottle and smashed off the bottom against the nightstand. I thought I was done for, but he dropped the broken bottle on the floor, laughing in my face, and sat up. Then, without warning, like an afterthought he commenced punching me in the head. No-one will buy you now, he sneered, not with a face like that. My head was bashing against the end of the bed as he hit me, and it was that which Magda heard, that and my yells, and she came in with her big knife in her hand. She couldn't get him, though, 'cause he used the broken bottle to keep her away whilst he pulled his clothes on. She was screaming for Tony but by the time he came up the stairs, the evil bastard was out the door. I heard him threaten Tony with the bottle."

The schadenfreude I'd enjoyed when hearing about Big Mac's arrest now tasted like vomit in my mouth as I recalled my earlier glee. I should have foreseen this. Was nothing good going to come from my windfall? Well, it had brought me closer to Rula, I couldn't deny that, but at what a price! And, strange though you might think it of me, remarking this at such a traumatic time, but Rula's account of the assault had struck me with its demonstration of her improved proficiency in spoken English. Out of suffering comes...what? I couldn't think of the word, I was too diverted by thoughts of my own impending suffering, for surely I'd now be a target for the McAllisters' revenge. My mind was in thrashing mode, I'd completely forgotten the two young whores who sat there clutching each other on the sofa. It was Magda who broke into my thoughts:

"What is she going to do, no man is going to want her while she looks like this. How will we pay the rent?"

Well, fuck the rent. Sometimes one has to let the right-hand side of one's brain take charge, even though I'm not usually driven by sentiment.

"Not to worry," I replied. "But best that Rula doesn't stay here while she recuperates."

I hope it wasn't brought about by my brain's left side, the overbearing bunch of neurons that do all the scheming and organisation, but when I arrived back home Sniffer had two of us to greet.

It was only natural, sitting in the conservatory after lunch, each with a glass of brandy and one of my home made cannabis cakes to nibble, that I should relate to Rula the outcome of my visit to Knock Hall.

"I told you," she exclaimed. "That posh woman, she is not nice. Now you tell me she has a collection of guns. Is she a terrorist, do you think? There are subversives in every country, hiding away, waiting for their time to come."

"But they're not her guns—or my father's, for that matter."

83

So then of course I had to tell her what I had found out about the Saltire organisation.

"This North East Chapter," she asserted, "it sounds to me like a private army. We have them in our country too, the people's militia they call themselves, but it's all a cover for drugs and people trafficking. A sort of mafia. Well, that's what most people say."

She had pulled a sour face whilst telling me this and, remembering the story of how she'd killed a man in Belarus, I wondered whether she'd had personal experience of these groups on her journey into prostitution.

"I don't believe my father was involved in such serious criminal activity," I responded, "just a spot of good, honest smuggling—you know, fine liquors, luxury cloths, that kind of thing."

"You are funny," she chuckled, "your English, talking about honest crime."

I wasn't going to explain English idiom, it was just encouraging to see her smiling again, so I continued with my story:

"So, somehow, the Saltire got wind of what my father and the Duchess's business comprised; perhaps a member of the North East Chapter was one of the merchantmen they unwittingly traded through. When it comes down to it, there are very few people you can trust in life. Whatever, the Saltire organisation had realised they'd stumbled upon an opportunity. They could use the old wharf and the tunnel to bring in the guns and store them. The tunnel was also a good safe place to keep their counterfeit cash. And once the river end of the tunnel collapsed there was only one point of access. My father and the Duchess weren't ever going to split on them, for obvious reasons, so they must have felt pretty secure with that arrangement. Which is more than I do right now," I added.

"We'll deal with this, how do you say, conundrum?" She took my hand.

"We?" I felt a stirring of unease. "But this is not your problem. You've been hurt already; I can't put you at further risk." I withdrew my hand to emphasise our separateness. "I'm going to find somewhere out of the way where you can stay until this is all over."

She looked hurt. "We'll deal with it together," she said firmly.

"Well, that in itself is a conundrum." And so it was, in more ways than one. "I'm impressed, by the way, how your language skills have come on…"

"Don't mock me," she said in a soft voice, standing up. She then bent and pressed her bruised lips upon mine. Like I said earlier, you never really know what a woman is thinking.

The deal was sealed and that, I suppose, is how I became shacked up with a prostitute. Many men would recoil at the idea. At one time, I would have been among them. Indeed, as a sanctimonious young teenager, on a particularly embarrassing occasion, I got on my moral high horse and declared to my father that prostitutes were the embodiment of wickedness and should be exterminated. He then made clear he was a left brain sort of man, calling me stupid and pointing out that without the services of prostitutes there'd be a lot more women attacked by men.

My attempt at moral rectitude had been nothing more than a sorry display of adolescent naivety, I could feel that even then, and his quick retort was perhaps the beginning of my sloughing off those extreme and outmoded conventions that had no basis in logic. That was long ago and I now understood that shacking up with Rula was no more nor less than what it was, acceptance of a beautiful and disarming young woman into my life as my amorous partner. Something I had been missing for a long time, I quickly came to realise.

But enough of all that sappy stuff. What were we going to do about what Rula had dubbed our conundrum? Sooner or later Ronnie was going to come knocking. I also had the Saltire to deal with, for at some point the Duchess was going to depart this world and I would become the custodian of several chests of military-grade weapons. For the moment, Rula decided what to do.

"Let's go for a walk," she said. "If we're not here, the terrible Mr McAllister won't find us. Anyway, it's a lovely sunny day, we shouldn't waste it."

With her spirit so evidently on the mend, I couldn't gainsay her. I was also keen to show her the attractions of my local environment, and in a short while, with Sniffer doing nose-paintings on the car's rear window, we were driving down the narrow road to the beach, parking up on the grass verge, as the car park was closed for renovation.

"We used to park here on what was a wild piece of land," I explained to Rula, "a rough space of grass and stones bounded by wild flowers—ox-eye daisies, devil's-foot scabious, with bluebells and daffodils in spring—somehow it was a fitting entrance to the rest of the wild and untamed coast over there beyond the dunes. Then some interfering do-gooders who'd moved here from the city rented the land and, offended by its untidiness and lack of management, they raised a lot of money to have the place turned into a regular car park with painted spaces and regulations, an arid desert with no natural ambience, and for the use of which they say we'll have to pay."

She looked at me. "You don't like people, do you?"

I laughed. "What are you then, an alien?"

We climbed to the top of the highest dune and sat looking out over the long empty beach below, while Sniffer chased rabbits in the marram grass.

"Wow!" she exclaimed, spotting the swarm of grey seals on their haul-out at the river's mouth. "This is fantastic. There must be…"

"About a thousand." The number still astonished me. "Many more than when we moved here, for in those days the fishermen who worked the shore were able to shoot them. But commercial fishing has now gone."

She nodded to give agreement to that fact. "It's lovely here," she remarked, peering with obvious puzzlement at the far side of the dunes, "but also lonely. One could hide away here, although I'm not suggesting we stay here to avoid that awful Ronnie. But, all the same, if he came here now, that's somewhere we could take cover. What is it?"

She was pointing down into the valley that separated the two main reaches of dunes where, on the furthest rise, an old redbrick World War Two pillbox sat unmoving in the midst of a liquid plateau of golden sand.

It had been part of the defences against expected German invasion, and I described to her how huge concrete blocks had also been installed along the top of the beach, to deter Nazi landing craft. If they managed to get over the blocks and around the end of the first tranche of dunes, the little pillbox, bristling with armaments, was meant to surprise them.

"But it never happened," I explained to Rula, "the invasion. I suppose the men waiting in this building with their machine guns must have been disappointed."

"Or relieved."

"Aye."

She looked for a while down into the valley. "It's a wild place. In a good sort of way," she conceded. "I expect it was fun to come here when you were a kid."

Her conjecture threw me back to my youthful adventures and in the developing glow of our friendship I was tempted to wax lyrical, although that is not my nature.

"In my teens, I would come here of an evening. There was a regular gathering on warm summer evenings, and no-one could see us. We would drink from bottles of McEwans and inhale from inexpertly rolled spliffs; hah, we thought we really were the business. The older boys, who didn't share my dread of STDs, would take turns in a quiet hollow to ride the village bicycle, it was that secluded a place. And it was too far from home for our parents to bother come looking; I suppose it allowed us a feeling of safe rebellion. It all seems a bit sordid now though, looking back, and there's a bit of a mess been left down there."

Looking back now I was also aware how peripheral I'd been, on the outside of whatever was going down, watching, evaluating, forming a web of thoughts that are with me now. I noticed she was watching me, waiting for my thought processes to conclude.

"I mean, if you go over to the pillbox today there's nothing but smashed bottles in the sand. But you're right, Rula, as younger kids we would hide in there and play war games, picking off the 'enemy' through the loopholes with our spud guns—you see those narrow windows, they've got metal shutters that still work."

She was, of course, fascinated and, despite my warning about broken glass, we had to go and see, sliding down an uncertain deer trail through stands of fireweed and thistle.

We'd just crossed the main track that ran between the two dune ridges when there came a shout, and we turned to see a man gesticulating and running down the slope the track followed at the end of the valley. "Hey!" he called, and something else that we couldn't make out. He looked heated and aggressive, running awkwardly because the sand was soft and deep, but he seemed determined to catch up with us.

"Is that him?" I blurted. "McAllister?" I'd only her description of him and couldn't make a match. I took out my gun and flicked off the safety.

Then I recognised the man. It was one of the village worthies behind the car park fiasco.

"Hey," he said, coming up breathlessly. "Your dog did a poo." He held up a doggy waste bag. "Here you are, I picked it up. You need to watch your dog you know, not let him run around unattended. It's an offence to leave dog waste."

I took the bag in silence. Then he saw the gun in my hand.

"I hope you have a licence for that," he said nervously, his tone no longer pompous.

"None of your business, is it?" I answered. "I carry it in case I encounter trouble with busybodies."

"Of course he has a licence," interjected Rula, squeezing my arm with warning. "We are on a humane mission, if we find rabbits infected with myxomatosis we can put them out of their misery."

"Oh," spluttered the man, "good work." And hurriedly he stumbled away.

I was laughing silently and Rula seemed puzzled.

"Marvellous of you," I grinned, "but completely wrong. The myxomatosis outbreak in Britain ran its course a long way back, in the 1950s. That dumbfuck doesn't know his modern history. Anyway, his ignorance saved him. If I'd imagined I was in a Tarantino film, he'd be lying here with a slug through his brain."

"Do you do that?" she asked. "Imagine what you just said?"

"All of the time," I laughed. "Come on, let's bury this bag of shit, it says it's made of corn starch not plastic. It'll degrade in a couple of months. There's much worse buried under this patch of sand, I can tell you. And, incidentally, where'd you dig up the word for that rabbit disease?"

She ignored my tease and we walked across the beach to the river so that she could take a closer look at the seals, who were providing an impromptu concert with their eerie wailing song and, having dissuaded Sniffer from carrying a dead rabbit all the way to the car, we were soon on our way back home.

"Does he often do that." asked Rula. She was clearly not very dog savvy after all.

"Often. It's okay, he knows dogs are not susceptible to myxomatosis."

I was glad we'd had that encounter with the idiot in the dunes. Grabbing the gun so readily, instinctively I suppose, it made me feel confident I could react quickly in the event we were confronted by Ronnie McAllister. As for the Tarantino quip, I'd seen all his films, my favourite being 'Reservoir

Dogs'. His characters' unquestioning instinct to shoot their way out of any difficulty, large or small, whilst exhibiting no qualms, had taken root somewhere in my inner consciousness. Mr White, Mr Pink, Mr Orange, Mr Blue, Mr Brown and Mr Blonde. I guessed they were the colours of snooker balls, with Blonde being yellow, although there was no Mr Green or Mr Black. I resisted calling myself Mr Black, despite that being my regular colour of dress, but the notion still clung in my mind and gave a little swagger to my step.

7

We waited around the house for three days, certain he would come, but although I kept the gun fully loaded there was no incident with a sharply dressed intruder. Contrary to expectations, our mood had become one of tetchy boredom.

"You know what?" I said to Rula, "when we see him, you should immediately demand the payment he owes you. You know, for services rendered. That'll throw him, put him on the back foot. The power of words can be as powerful as a gun. It's like a saying you may have heard, that the pen is mightier than the sword. We can use the spoken word to break his focus, give us time to get our blows in first."

I thought I was being clever, but in retrospect it was a bit silly, an outcome of my mood. What I'd suggested was a ploy I'd relied upon, all those years ago, at school: introduce a moment of dissociation in order to whack a bully in the face or kick him in the privates before he remembered he wanted to thump me. Trouble is, Ronnie McAllister was a good deal more dangerous than a school bully.

"That all sounds very smart but I'd rather just forget the whole encounter," she said dismally. "Only of course he isn't going to let us forget it, is he? Let's just stay with our plan."

We'd been arguing over what to do if Ronnie turned up at my house and talk between us was beginning to turn fractious, probably out of a buried sense of worry. My T-shirt, of all things, had become pivotal to a silly quarrel between us. It was one of my favourites and bore the cryptic slogan 'Sorry, I…' followed by the depiction of four guitar chord shapes.

"That's stupid," had snapped Rula, staring at it. "What does it mean? It doesn't mean anything, it's stupid."

"It just doesn't mean anything to you," I answered without explaining the shapes. "Which actually says something about you."

I wasn't being helpful, I know, just irritatingly didactic. I can be such an awkward bastard. But that comment turned up the temperature and she threw her drinking glass into the sink with a crash.

Fortunately for our relationship it was at that precise moment there came a hearty knock on the front door and we both leapt to our feet.

As we'd planned, Rula crept out of the kitchen door in order to go around the house from the side, throwing down her sling as she slunk out, whilst I went stealthily to open at the front, my gun loaded and ready, and with Sniffer shut safely in the kitchen. He was of course barking his head off, as he does at every knock at the door, which gave away that someone was at home.

"Good day," said the man on the step, leaning forward, his face in mine, and stupidly I dropped the gun in surprise. So much for Mr Black! But from his confidently cheery smile this clearly wasn't Ronnie McAllister. I wondered how he managed that smile without discomfort, for he had a fiery ragged scar from his mouth to his ear. "I'm Alan Mackie, how

93

do you do?" he said for introduction, putting out his hand. "Your new—"

He didn't finish, for at that gesture of a well-meant handshake, probably mistaken as threatening, I caught a glimpse of Rula flying feet first through the air like some glamorous Ninja, her wild cry of 'yaaaa!' sufficient to stop Sniffer's barking, back in the kitchen. She caught my visitor, Alan, on the shoulder, as he bent to retrieve my gun from the doormat, and instead he stumbled back onto the lawn, where she momentarily pinned his arms behind his back, then as quickly released him.

It was all more like a Marvel movie scene than the tense Tarantino spectacle I had anticipated playing out.

"This is not him," Rula called, with a frown of disappointment and, pulling Alan to his feet, offered a quick-witted plea of, "terribly sorry, I thought you were the dognapper." Brushing him down with her long fingers she propelled him towards the front door, where I was scrabbling for the wayward gun.

Together, we bundled him inside and, to cover my embarrassment, I offered him the last of my brandy. That's when he explained that he was Walter's replacement, my new go-between with the Saltire organisation, as he believed Major Frisk had promised, but come sooner than I'd expected. He appeared to be more amused than angry at his rough reception, and I got the feeling that this was someone who was familiar with irregular conduct.

"So, how is it that dealing with a dognapper requires a handgun and an assistant proficient in martial arts, are the felons coming tooled-up these days?" Alan was laughing.

"It's a long story," I answered. "Please accept our apologies for the exceptionally enthusiastic greeting."

"Indeed," he said. "Lucky you didn't point that thing at me." I'd placed my gun on the kitchen table and he nudged it with a forefinger. "It would have been like gunfight at the old corral out there." So saying, he eased a long-barrelled pistol from a hidden holster under his blouson and waved it at me. "What would the neighbours have thought?"

It hadn't been a consideration, and I wondered too if anyone had witnessed Rula assaulting an unknown caller with a flying kick. But him revealing that he personally came 'tooled up' was a significant statement, one that I told myself I'd need to give greater thought when he'd gone.

"Don't tell me," he said, seeing me watching him reholster the gun. Then, answering his own question and pointing at my T-shirt, "you really don't give a fuck, do you? Brave man. Major Frisk told me to expect a cool customer."

I knew then that we were going to get on, him and me, for he'd declared himself a fellow guitarist. Like I said, I was wearing my favourite T-shirt with its cryptic slogan completed by the chord shapes for D, G, A and F. He'd clocked it immediately.

"What do you play?" he asked, and we entered into a lively dispute concerning the relative attributes of Fender versus Gibson guitars, which had Rula's eyes quickly rolling with boredom.

"Excuse me," she said, at long last, "but please, would you mind telling me why you are here, only we have a lot to deal with at the moment." And pointedly she removed the almost empty bottle of brandy so that he would not become more voluble.

"So," said Alan, sitting back as though ready to provide an answer, although he didn't. Just a question: "What is it that you are having to deal with?" he asked. "It sounds like something grave is weighing upon you. Of course, my concern has only to be whether it has anything to do with Saltire business; in which case, naturally, my interest would be aroused. After all, I didn't expect to be coming here to be assaulted by one of the Furies or find my trusted curator of Saltire assets waving a gun in my face."

"I wasn't exactly waving…" I felt, and probably looked, sheepish saying that.

But I didn't really want to tell him our story, for obviously it would mean referring to the disposition of Saltire property. Not so Rula who, being such an open person, she jumped straight in to explain how we were hiding from a brute who wanted revenge for his brother's mistake in handling dodgy banknotes that he'd stolen from us.

Alan was quick on the uptake and quickly put two and two together. Or so he seemed to do for a second or two.

"So, the dognapper was fiction," he began.

"No," Rula responded, "there is a dognapper—"

We were poised on the fringe of a verbal muddle and I rather rudely but gently clapped a hand over her mouth, receiving a swipe in return.

"Okay," Alan put his hand on her wrist. "Let the guitar-playing male chauvinist explain, please."

So I told him enough to make sense, which was less than half of the story, focusing on what Rula had given away to Ronnie McAllister.

"Then our merchandise is at risk, is it not?" He no longer wore his cheery smile. "Major Frisk told me the store is virtually impregnable, but I want to take a look for myself if I'm to bear any responsibility for its security. We'll make this my initial inspection, checking the inventory, so to speak."

"The money?" I feared he'd want to examine the visibly depleted suitcases.

"It's all crap," he answered. "Useless. You have my permission to burn it. No, I'd like to see the actual merchandise. You know what I mean, don't you?"

I wondered how the Duchess would take to our appearance so soon after the visit with Benny, but I had little choice. Rula insisted on accompanying us, which was sure to complicate matters given she'd already taken against the 'nasty Frenchwoman', but I didn't want a row in front of the man from Saltire and we all squeezed into Rula's bright blue Porsche. I say we all squeezed in, but it was only me who was sat up behind the pair of them, wedged between the two head restraints. Good job I don't stand on dignity.

"You okay to drive," I asked pointing at Rula's blackened eye, which was still half closed. Her answer was to floor the accelerator, and I only managed to stay put because of Alan's firm hands around my ankles. After her slap, was she telling me something?

There was an ostentatiously tricked out yellow car parked on the drive at Knock Hall, a car sporting a ridiculously wide tailpipe that I remembered immediately. Someone was slouched in the driver's seat enveloped by a deafening episode of rap that seemed to pound the air around the vehicle like some kind of protective forcefield. The jarring noise increased my sense of antipathy towards the occupant, a young man with a shaved head. His appearance from the car, when he saw us emerge from the Porsche, did little to calm me.

"Oi, you nobs," was his greeting. "You can't go in there."

"And why, pray, is that?" coolly enquired Alan. "We are here for a business engagement with the lady of the house, and I don't think we intend to be sent away by a bumptious little scrote like yourself."

The kid reddened at that. "Don't you know who I am?" he bristled. "I'm a McAllister, an' my stepdad's in there already." His unprompted announcement resonated with uncertain bravado. "He's here on important business and he told me he's not to be interrupted."

"Look, sonny," said Alan. "See that nice blue car in which we arrived? Which would you prefer, that or your yellow monstrosity?"

The kid looked puzzled. What was this bloke talking about? What a stupid question.

"Well mine, of course. Ultimate babe magnet, that one…" He spat across the drive to point out Rula's vehicle. "That blue one's for old men and posh tarts, wouldn't have any street cred for the likes of me."

Alan walked around to the front of the young man's vehicle and kicked in the headlamps. "I expect you're tempted now to do the same to our car," he taunted, seeing the kid's look of angry intent. "But," he continued, taking out his long-barrelled gun, "some impulses are best left unanswered. Now fuck off!"

The kid hesitated and Alan raised the gun as if taking aim. "Your stepdad, is that Ronnie McAllister by any chance?"

He nodded, and sensing this situation was resolving into something bigger than he had at first imagined, opened his car door.

"Go on then," urged Alan, "piss off, if you're going to."

"B…but," stammered the kid, "I'm his ride. He told me to wait for him so—"

"Don't worry," Alan assured him, "we'll take care to get him where he's going. Goodbye."

We stood and watched as the vulgar yellow car rumbled off noisily onto The Avenue, and I felt a grudging admiration for Alan's no-nonsense handling of the situation.

"But," said Rula, catching him by the wrist. "Suppose he hadn't anything to do with the McAllisters and he only pretended he was, just to brag and scare you, they're quite infamous; and suppose he really was just innocently waiting for his dad? Some other dad."

Alan smiled and tapped his nose with a forefinger. "But he wasn't. One gets a nose for such things. Anyway, he told us without having to tell us."

I was disappointed in myself. Alan had played a far more convincing Mr Black than I probably would have done in the circumstances. It's not just having the gun; one has to have attitude as well. I determined to do better. And also to remember that Alan's boots had steel toecaps.

"I enjoyed that," I admitted, gently punching his arm. "But why such extravagance? He was no threat, was he?"

Some of Alan's smile returned, albeit with a sardonic curl. "I loathe rap," he explained. "Low black music—or not music at all when it comes down to it."

Mrs Delacroix's front door was ajar. As a precaution, we didn't knock but pushed it open. Something heavy grated across the tiled entrance floor and I picked up her shotgun, which was jamming the door.

"Careless," muttered Alan. But Mrs Delacroix was, I felt, far from being the careless type.

"It's a warning," I suggested.

"Or she was attempting to use it." Rula completed our thoughts.

We made our way through the house, nothing appearing to have been moved since I was here with Benny. The air in the room with the bay window was as chilly as ever.

"Don't tell me she's a biker," remarked Alan, pointing to the leather jacket and pants thrown over the table.

"She's not. But seeing that suggests to me she's probably in serious trouble."

With that thought uppermost, I hurried them into and down the long hallway that led to the tunnel entrance. The door at the end was open and we could hear distant echoey voices. Taking the steps quietly, I saw the lights come on overhead and thought how we needn't try to be quiet; the lights would give us away anyway.

But there was another brightness ahead and I remembered the flashlight which, as we neared, I could make out was standing up-ended on the sandy floor. Its bright beam, reflecting off the ceiling, cancelled out the advancing presence of our own light. That floor too made a hush of our footsteps.

We could now hear a man's rough voice, presumably Ronnie McAllister's and, momentarily, Rula hung back. Then she made a fist of resolve and pushed to take the lead, at which Alan caught her arm and shook his head, easing his gun from its holster to reassure her of his own intentions, then letting it drop back.

Drawing near we could see that McAllister had one of the coffers open and was rummaging inside. Before long, he stood up, triumphantly waving some kind of gun in one hand,

and turned to the Duchess, who had pressed herself against the tunnel wall. She was dressed only in her underwear and was visibly shivering. From the chill or from fear, it was impossible to tell. She'd never seemed like a woman who'd allow herself to be intimidated, but...

"Come on, bitch, pass me some ammo," barked McAllister, still unaware of our approach.

Her movements stiffened by fear, the Duchess shuffled over to the adjacent coffer and loosed the lid, retrieving a package wrapped in oilcloth, which he snatched from her, ripping open the covering so carelessly that the contents fell to the floor with a thud.

"Pick it up," we heard him demand, which was when I saw the wicked-looking serrated knife that he was brandishing at her.

She handed him a black, shiny magazine and he rammed it into the stock of the gun he was holding, an assault rifle I guessed, a more complicated-looking example than I had seen before. Unexpectedly, he threw down his knife and pointed the gun at her, the Duchess giving a short cry; but he just laughed, aimed the gun into the distant gloom of the tunnel, and let off a volley of shots.

What happened next was, I thought then and still do, wholly bizarre. Either Alan has an overblown sense of his superiority, he's a complete show-off, or he is barking mad. For, instead of shooting the bastard, as I had confidently anticipated, he stepped forward stealthily and clamped his arm around McAllister's throat from behind, pulling him backwards, a knee in his back, his other hand reaching for the rifle. Several further shots blew chips of stone out of the ceiling as McAllister wrestled to keep hold of his weapon.

Having experienced Alan's strength in the car—my ankles were sore!—I was sure the thug would quickly be overpowered, but he managed to wriggle around, all the time trying to bring the muzzle of his gun up towards Alan's body.

They both had a hold of the rifle now and the struggle had become a pure trial of strength. I felt myself fascinated, like a spectator at a public wrestling match.

"Give me my gun," I heard Alan say, as cool as ever.

"Yeah, I'll give it to you," came the gruff reply, and a shot rang out, sending Alan hopping backwards across the tunnel, whilst Ronnie McAllister raised the rifle once more, with Alan in his sights.

That of course was my cue to turn from being an onlooker to a participant, so I took my own gun in my hand and shot McAllister in the stomach. To be final it should have been in the head, I know, but after what he'd done to Rula I wanted him to suffer. Death from a slug in the belly is slow and painful.

I ran to Alan who was being hugged by a half-naked Mrs Delacroix. He swayed on one leg, having been shot in the foot.

"I can deal with this," said the Duchess. "Let's get you back upstairs," and Alan was instantly made to hobble away, leaning on her shoulder. I wasn't sure whether her desire for haste was because of her concern for him or due to her embarrassment at being seen undressed like that. I must say, it wasn't a pretty sight for a young man like me to see, with that puckered belly and shrivelled musculus pectoralis, it made me wonder where had gone the robustly confident dominatrix in black leather I'd seen but a short while ago. Crumbs, if our national leaders were made to go naked they'd not be able to exercise any of their pompous authority.

But back to the moment, where all was not over, for my eyes were diverted to the new scene being played out on the sandy floor. Rula had acted with alacrity, evidence of her arm injury gone, and taking hold of McAllister's knife, rapidly cut away his belt and trousers with its cruel blade. She now deftly removed his underpants, which were already drenched with dark red blood. He was conscious but unable to struggle, his legs seeming to have lost the power of movement. Instead, he beat his arms on the floor and issued a torrent of curses from his spittle-flecked mouth, calling Rula every variation on the theme of filthy whore.

For a moment, I thought she was going to remove his manhood; and so, I imagine did he. She even grabbed it for a moment and tugged, making him roar with pain and fear until she slapped his face hard and spoke loudly into it.

"Remember," she asked, "what you were threatening to do with that bottle in my apartment? Where you were going to put it?"

He looked at her with a stupefied lack of understanding. At her next words, he was fully in the picture and his roar turned to screams, "I don't have a bottle with me," she continued, "although I do have your knife, and I'm going to put it where the sun don't shine."

I don't know where she'd picked up her English idiom, perhaps from Benny, which would be ironic given his origins, but she did exactly as she'd threatened, turning the knife so that the blade could fully exercise its devilish irregularities in the pungent darkness of his rectum.

There's no revenge like that of a wronged woman, and the look in her eyes as she stood and turned to me made it very clear that I would have to treat her with extreme caution in future. No more male chauvinism, unintended or not.

"Two minutes," she said, watching McAllister writhe on the sandy floor. "Give me two minutes. Let me relish what I have done, then you can finish him. After all, you're the man with the gun, aren't you?"

Her confidence—and her grasp of English—had rallied considerably. Relish indeed!

When McAllister had finally been despatched to whatever place in hell awaited him, we had of course to dispose of the body. I did wonder if we could just leave him there, on the floor, I was keen to get away. In that atmosphere, in time his remains would desiccate. But people from the Saltire would be coming here periodically and they'd not want to be tripping over a corpse. We had to move it.

"Down there," suggested Rula, pointing away down the passage, "where the roof's fallen in, that might be a good place."

We made our way along to where the stability of the tunnel wall seemed very ambiguous. The reinforced concrete that had lined the walls and ceiling had split and crumbled, exposing great expanses of bare hewn granite. Debris was strewn increasingly across the floor, rough chunks of rock and metal, and the coffers that continued to line the passageway there were dented and misshapen. Gradually the space between roof and floor decreased, with a huge bulging ingress of rock pressing down from above. It looked as though the furthest coffers were actually supporting the tunnel roof, and at this point in our gradual descent there came the ominous sound of water dripping.

"This is where she expects we'll come to retrieve our own goods," I muttered, contemptuously, "the stuff that she and my father brought here." I still had only a vague idea of what it might comprise. "I wouldn't want to shift this lot though, not without proper equipment, however valuable the contents." It would be a reckless soul who attempted inexpertly to pull these containers free of a looming rock roof, which had already staked its claim upon them. Yet the container immediately next to where we'd stopped was undamaged, despite the boulders in the roof hanging precariously above it.

"Let's take a look," Rula suggested, and dutifully I shot the coffer's lock to pieces. A bit of a daft thing to do, actually, as it caused a torrent of shingle, then fine sand, to escape from between the shifting rocks above. A torrent that eventually slowed to a trickle but did not entirely cease, it made a swishing noise like falling water as it fell upon the exposed glass necks of the brandy bottles that, lifting the lid, we now saw stacked in layers inside the coffer. I eased one from its straw sheaf; it was good stuff, I knew that, and the whole consignment would have sold for a tidy price.

"Come on," I urged Rula. "Help me unload this lot, will you."

It took us the best part of an hour to take out all the bottles and carry them, two at a time, back up to a safer part of the tunnel. Finally, leaning in to complete our task, wedged between the bottom layer of bottles and the side of the container I discovered a yellowed document, which on examination proved patently to be an old ship's manifest. It was stamped with the vessel's name: Glad Rose.

"There," I exhaled with noisy glee, my fatigue lifted by the find. "As we surmised, all those names on the dockets in the loft: the names of boats."

When Rula hauled out the last two bottles and stopped to take breath, I beat my fist on the empty coffer, making it boom like a bass drum. "McAllister's last resting place," I announced, and she grinned.

Despite us both feeling dog tired, we grasped the corpse by the ankles, and dragged his body the length of the tunnel, all the way to the emptied coffer. Or should I say coffin? The look fixed on McAllister's cold thin face was, we both agreed, one of incredulity. My own thoughts were wearing an edge of astonishment at all that had taken place, I must admit, and once we'd tumbled the corpse inside the coffer, I stood for a while, my mind adrift, for long seconds truly in a mist. Rula nudged me: "Having second thoughts about this?"

No, my thoughts were crystallising.

"Just thinking. Mrs Delacroix reckoned it was 100% safe here, or near enough, since no-one was likely to make their way down here other than Saltire people. But Ronnie McAllister managed in, didn't he? So who else might one day get down here and…"

"Find the body!" she squealed.

"Just wait here a minute," I called, nodding, already hastening back up the passage.

Returning quickly, and with the semi-automatic Ronnie had pulled from the first coffer braced against my chest, I aimed at the ceiling directly above his tomb, holding back the trigger so that a rapid spray of shells slammed into the loosened stones above us.

The recoil from the gun was like a hammer blow in my shoulder, and the potent energy it threw from the barrel caused rocks to fall instantly, but they dropped only piecemeal; where I had expected a major collapse the fall seemed just to pepper the coffer lid. This was no good. I fired again, one very long burst, and there came a shower of sand, more rocks and an eerie metallic tearing as granite scraped against granite and the outer metal casing of the passage buckled behind the stones above us.

All that weight and suspended dynamics up there really scared me, and we speedily retreated a safe distance. I thought at that moment of the great sum of money my father must have contributed to have engineers construct and seal this tunnel against the volatile geology outside, then I heard a roar as the roof collapsed under the weight of centuries of sand. The roar grew and sustained as the light dimmed and more and more of the tunnel ahead of us buckled and caved in until, stepping back when it had quietened, we peered through a haze of dust to find ourselves facing a formidable wall of stones and twisted steel. The secret way to the old wharf was definitely no more; more importantly, Ronnie's last resting place was no longer visible, although it was but several meters away from us. Sadly, so too was lost any chance of ever retrieving whatever treasures had been secreted down there. It was now buried treasure in the truest sense.

"Come on," I urged Rula, "I've had enough of this place."

I bent and snatched up a bottle of brandy as we toiled up the sloping passageway. "Something needs celebrating," I explained. "Although I'm not exactly sure what that something is just yet."

Alan was sitting on a plump cushion in the wide bay window when we emerged from our subterranean adventure. He had regained some of his cheery countenance and his foot was bound in a clean white bandage. Mrs Delacroix sat at the table, her head propped in her hands; she jumped to her feet when we came through the door.

"Thank goodness," she exclaimed. "When I heard all that rumbling, I imagined you'd both come a cropper."

'But you didn't come to see, did you, come see if we were in trouble?' That was my private thought. "No, that was us," I explained, "just hiding the evidence. No-one will know he was there—although you might go down and clear up the blood in the sand, if you've a moment. Just in case."

"That vile man. He told me he was from the Council, something about revaluation for Council Tax. Pushed his way in. Made me strip—oh that knife!—I thought I was going to be raped."

My mind went back to the picture of her standing there in her underwear, her old flesh white and stringy, the flattened breasts. Surely he wouldn't have, would he? But there's no accounting for taste.

"He had other more pressing thoughts on his mind," I reassured her. "And it's all over now, anyway."

"There's still that lad," interjected Alan. "He's going to wonder where his dad has got to in an hour or so. Someone will come asking questions."

"His chauffeur? That toe-rag, he's hardly likely to report him missing to the police," observed the Duchess.

"I wasn't thinking of the police coming to find him," was my two-pennyworth. No, I imagined the McAllisters had a

108

whole cohort of thugs and villains who would rally round at a time like this.

"Don't worry," said Alan, "I'm going to remain here for a while. Mrs Delacroix has a medic she knows coming to see to my wounded foot—confidentially, of course. I shall stay here a couple of days to recuperate. Anybody comes sniffing around, I think we can deal with them." He took out his gun and checked the magazine. "Anyway, we might well be having reinforcements. But, all the same, you two watch out for boy racers in pimped up yellow cars."

It was a good point. The kid would have remembered Rula's car if not our faces.

"Let's get back." It now felt urgent. "Rula, you can put your conspicuous wagon in my garage for the time being. Out of sight." I picked up the bottle of brandy from the table where I'd set it down. "There's plenty more of this down there," I said to Alan. "Do help yourself to a bottle."

"As I intimated, I'm expecting company," answered Alan. "the North East Chapter is going on exercises. I've already cleared it with our lady host, they can camp here. My men might be thirsty."

He said it jokingly, but I wasn't bothered anyway. I could buy all the brandy I wanted with my stash from the loft. For now, I just wanted to be safe. Old brandy has nothing special to offer apart from its intrinsic quality of taste, since spirits don't improve with age, so Alan's men could take whatever they wanted.

8

Rula seemed to have regained her poise by taking her revenge on Ronnie McAllister. As she drove us home I was tempted to conjecture just how it was she'd been so quickly overcome when he attacked her, for clearly she was no fainthearted weakling. I'd read a little about victim syndrome and wondered whether she had simply had a spasm of mental incapacity. The condition is identifiable as a personality trait whereby an individual tends to recognise or consider themselves a victim of the negative actions of others. But that is usually in a different context, the dark world of domestic abuse, the case of battered wives for example. As a prostitute, Rula's working life would have been continuous hell if she truly suffered from that syndrome. So maybe the answer was simple, Ronnie's display of violence had proved just too overpowering at the time, an instance of shock and awe. I remembered how much of a fight he'd put up against Alan, who was no feeble sissy by the look (and feel) of him. Well, whatever had gone down, McAllister had paid the price, so good on the lass!

But I was feeling a little prickly by the time we reached the house, and not even Sniffer's extravagant greeting seemed to elevate my mood. There were still questions I wanted to explore more satisfactorily with the Duchess; principally, why she had really gone to the extreme of including the Saltire as a beneficiary of her estate. I know she'd offered an explanation, but what she'd said about taking revenge had seemed too glib, even though it was clear to my mind that they had imposed their presence upon her through the exercise of duress, a simplistic wall of threat at least, before managing to deposit their considerable cache of weapons beneath her house.

I suggested we invite Benny to dinner and Rula was glad to concur. I felt bad that I hadn't been in touch for a few days. After all, he was probably the only man I could describe as a friend, and I didn't want to shut him out from all the drama that was going on. Or so I told myself; but if I'm to be honest, I just craved the indulgence of his good company as an antidote to the less agreeable events of the day.

Together we prepared a vegan goulash with jackfruit, big beans and mixed grains, and I opened the bottle of brandy. Benny brought a fine Italian Pinot Grigio, which we put on ice for a refreshing pre-prandial.

Sitting at the table while the goulash bubbled, with neither Benny nor I comfortable with small talk, he nudged me at last and said, "Here, I've got a funny story for you."

I nodded him to continue, which he did.

"There was this priest—"

"Ah," I interrupted. "I bet I know this one. There was a priest, a rabbi and a witchdoctor met in a pub—"

"No, no, no," he exclaimed, "not that kind of funny story but a curious tale. At least, I thought it curious, you'll no doubt find it educative."

"Go on, Benny, there will be no more interruptions." Rula gave me one of her looks.

"Well," Benny began again, "it's what Magda told me, about a client she had this week."

We both leaned in to hear him.

"It was a priest," said Benny, with a faux reverential air.

"Well I never." I had a feeling this was going to be tasty.

"That's what I said," agreed Benny, "although I shouldn't have been surprised, knowing what the clergy get up to back in Italy. Well, they concluded their transaction, all very civilised apparently, when he suddenly broke down and cried. Right there, sobbing, sitting up in the bed."

Of course, Magda at first thought she'd failed to satisfy him and asked what more he needed. "What I need is absolution," he blubbered, "but you cannot give it and I cannot ask it of the church. Not now, it's been so long."

"Magda tried to comfort him without knowing what was wrong, and at last his reticence broke and he commenced to pour it all out. 'I'm a sex addict,' he confessed. 'It started in my youth, in the Swinging Sixties. It was everywhere, sex; it's the basis for all of popular culture, of course, and popular culture was in the ascendance then. You'll know, I'm sure, that the words rock'n'roll themselves were a description for the sex act. And I was a fervent devotee of rock'n'roll. I was starting a foundation theology degree for the ministry at a time when it was all around us. Just think of the music of the time: the Stones' 'Let's Spend the Night Together', the Beatles' 'Please Please Me'. All about fucking. And fucking's what dominated my student days. Overwhelmingly so.'"

"Hang on a minute, did he explain about the Beatles?" I was intrigued.

112

"No," said Benny, "but surely you've always wondered about it. Four nice scouse lads with broad smiles and cute haircuts, that's how they were sold, but they'd just had an extended period of debauchery in Germany, and they were urging the girl in the song to come on, come on, please please me, and she didn't need to be shown how."

"Oh come on, Benny, that's not right, surely." I was laughing.

"Rula, how about you?" he appealed.

She sat, speechless and bemused.

"I'm not sure western popular culture made it very far into the Soviet bloc," I tried to explain. "But do go on about the priest."

"Well, his story was that he'd continued as he had begun, in parallel to his induction into the faith, and the further he went the harder it was to back out of what had become his cultural norm."

"Yes, but Magda, what did she do?"

"Oh Magda, she's got a head on her. She got up, put on her robe, and went to fetch Tony. As you may remember, Tony is an ex-Professor of Religious Studies. He came up and sat with the priest and explained the differences between different faiths towards sex. After a long hour or more, the priest got out of bed and declared he was going to switch his religious allegiance and become a Buddhist monk. He told Tony quite sincerely that saffron had always been his favourite colour."

At that, Rula and I, lubricated by the wine, almost fell off our chairs. It was a hilarious story and Benny had done just what I had hoped he would, pulling a fog of concealment over our worries.

113

"When did you make that up?" I asked. "Just now?"

"So there was no priest," said Rula, still somewhat mystified.

"Oh, but there was," confirmed Benny. "And he's bringing his novitiate with him next time for a threesome."

That was a good time to break and serve up the goulash.

"So," said Rula, cutting into the silence at the table (I told you Benny and I were hopeless at small talk), "how's the money laundering going, Benny?"

"Slowly," he slurped, "but surely. It's a lot to shift."

It was hardly a great conversation starter. Then Benny seemed to be struck by a thought, asking: "Remind me, how much was it you found up in your loft?"

"Twelve million in Sterling, plus a tidy sum in Euros."

"Ever wonder how he made that much, your father? Twelve million is a big deal after all. It's the kind of sum big players pull in and, don't take this for disrespect, 'cos I loved the man, but your dad was never that big a player. Remember, I did look over his accounts for him; but it was never obvious what he was importing, only the names of suppliers. I do recall thinking some of the item descriptions on the later shipping paperwork sounded a little odd, but nothing to pore over. All I was concerned about was keeping those HMRC robbers at arm's length." He munched on thoughtfully for a moment or too, then cried out with excitement, "Eureka, è fatta!"

Rula and I dropped our forks in surprise, which soon turned to puzzlement. "What?" we demanded in unison.

"Like I said, I always thought it was too much," he began. "Importing good wines and finery for those with money to spend and a blind eye to draw, and maybe the occasional kilo of skunk, it would have to have been wrapped in leaves of gold to produce that kind of profit. Notwithstanding the amount they were in hock for having that tunnel constructed or reinforced or whatever they did." He looked at me, clearly expecting a light to come on in my brain. "You're not there yet are you?" he grinned and patted my leg. "Their wines and cloth business—a great camouflage." He gave me a look to prompt my thoughts, and failed, sighing, "Oh well, someone who didn't cotton on to what 'Please Please Me' was all about is never going to get this one."

I sat back, feeling a little slighted and he noticed.

"My friend," he said, "I did wonder if it was drugs—you know, serious drugs—but he wouldn't have approved, and your dad was the senior partner in their business, as we've heard. Mary Jane maybe, but not the serious stuff. No, it was the guns, don't you see? That's how they made that great sum of money. It's not what the old lady said at all, the Saltire people didn't 'get wind' of their enterprise and muscle in on them; and they hadn't already exactly made their fortunes, like she admitted, her and your father. The two of them were importers, that much of what she said was true; they were doing okay, I knew that from your dad's accounts, but later in their career they saw a bigger opportunity; I suppose they got greedy. That's when they expanded into importing weapons—for the Saltire. That's how they made such a tidy sum in cash. But with it they'd become so involved, they were forced into maintaining a storage facility that they couldn't declare to the world."

It all made such sense now. Clever old Benny, he has that sort of mind, mathematical, taking all the data and rearranging it in his head until he has found a working algorithm or what have you.

"Okay. If that is what was going on, I'm actually somewhat relieved, for it means the money upstairs is legitimately mine to inherit, not the Saltire's. Major Frisk had not come to inspect the money after all; I recall now he'd referred to the 'merchandise'."

"Exactly," confirmed Benny.

"But," interjected Rula, who'd followed all of this quietly. "Why, if the Saltire organisation were simply clients, are they on the posh woman's will thing?"

That too was falling into place. "I think I can work that one out," I said, before Benny could explain. "My father was the initial beneficiary, then me, then my brother. Doing that she'd cleverly keep the secret of what kind of business had been going on—not least the importation and store of weaponry—in the family. Our family. And there's no way we were going to broadcast their years of illegal business, were we? As for admitting we were responsible for a store of guns and various pieces of contraband, well, what crimes wouldn't we have been deemed to commit? We'd probably be arrested as terrorists and sent to the English government's concentration camp in Rwanda. So far, she'd gambled on family loyalties."

"But after us—Dad, me and my brother—if we weren't alive, it had to be the Saltire, since it was all their terrible merchandise down there under the house. The Duchess was doubly under pressure, from them as well as from fear of discovery, to keep it hidden. And so would we be. They relied on that, but if the estate had been sold to someone else, how would the Saltire have recovered what they'd purchased for such big bucks? Imagine it all being found by a new owner, there'd be police and special branch all over the place. The name Beachborough would become synonymous with rebellion and uprisings, something we haven't seen hereabouts since the 1740s. And it would stymie whatever plans the Saltire have for those guns."

"Hmmm," mused Benny, "what plans do they have, I wonder? You ought to know, given that you are now lined up to be some kind of custodian for them."

It was a question I wasn't sure I wished to pursue, but it settled there in my brain with a small silent muscular contraction.

All this talk of guns and the Delacroix estate brought us back to the events of the day. Magda had told Benny the whole story of the assault on Rula and Rula was keen to reveal the corollary—namely, the tale of her revenge. I suppose it was what she needed to achieve a final closure.

We poured glasses of the excellent brandy I'd recovered and went through to the conservatory, sitting in the late evening Scottish sunshine whilst Rula related the earlier events up at Knock Hall. She spoke fluently in English, with barely a trace of her Slavic tongue, and I silently congratulated her with a smile and encouraging nod, while Benny responded to every twist and turn of her story with a grimace or frown, screwing up his shoulders and legs when she spoke with a certain delicious glee of the use to which she'd put Ronnie's knife.

"Oh God," he exclaimed, raising his fists to his ears, "it gets you right here."

"No," she laughed, "it was somewhere entirely different."

117

That brought lewd guffaws and the tension that had kept Benny on the edge of his seat was broken.

"So," he said to me, when she had at last finished, "you've lost all the goods your father and the Duchess had stored down there. That's a shame."

It was, perhaps, given it represented much of my dad's life's work. But here I was, a man previously of modest means at most, now with a loft still full of cash, as well as being the future inheritor of a significant estate. I'm not going to be sentimental over what had become buried under several tons of rock and sand.

"I can live with it," was all I said in answer.

"We'll be fine," chimed in Rula.

Hmmm, so we really are a 'we' now, are we? Was that something I had seriously considered in my more reflective moments? I made no comment. Time will tell, of course, unruly time with its unpredictably everchanging present, and I was quite happy with the present, actually, sitting there with two friends and a warming glass of cognac.

"All's well then," suggested Benny, I could hear the brandy in his voice. "We've sorted the whole puzzle surrounding your windfall."

I sat up with a start. "The puzzle, yes I agree, but I'm still entangled with the Saltire organisation; and, perhaps more worryingly, there's also the question of the McAllisters and the vanished stepfather."

"You need to lay low for a bit. This is far more difficult than dealing with Big Oil." Benny shook his head. "Forget the Saltire, I dare say they're no threat to you, but the McAllisters...Lay low."

118

9

The McAllisters were only the half of it. Rula was behaving as though she'd taken up residence. She showed no sign of wanting to leave, although her visible injuries were fast clearing up, and her mental recuperation seemed complete. Every day she accompanied Sniffer and me on our long morning walks and seemed exhilarated by the quiet outdoors. "I like it here," she said. "I like being with you." Well, fine, I was pleased that she was enjoying our time together. Then came the love word and I knew it was time for her to move on.

What is it with women? You meet someone with whom you like to spend time, you find them amusing, intelligent and attractive, the sex is mutually agreeable, and you get along easily. Isn't that enough for them? Time and again I've found that it isn't. They always spoil the magic by wanting commitment. Well, okay, I have no problem with commitment, being absolutely serious about us having good times together, I've no problem with that. But the rest, the declarations of undying devotion, sharing a toothbrush?

Not so long ago I had an affair with a woman who was a fellow dog walker. Our paths frequently crossed on the beach and, fatefully, we got talking. Matters quickly developed and,

119

I am very happy to remember, the sex was possibly the best I have enjoyed. Then, just a few weeks in, she declared that she was in love with me. Well, I ignored it for a while; if she wanted to think about it in that way I wasn't inclined to have an argument about it. So on we went, and the arrangement continued to be great fun, until after quite a while, a couple of months or more as I recall, she sat up in bed and announced that she was going to leave her husband and two children and get a divorce so that she could be with me all the time. Christ, I hadn't known she was married with kids until then, she was still pretty well upholstered and I'd never have guessed. She couldn't bear the secrecy, she explained, not any longer, she wanted it all out in the open. I didn't get it. As far as I was concerned, secrecy is all part of the excitement in a clandestine affair. After all, that's why we have affairs, isn't it, for the excitement, the adventure? Well, that was the end of it all, sadly, and I had to exclude the beach for a while from my regular round of walks with Sniffer.

Of course, I've been in love, but I know it for what it is— it's a hormonal thing that in prosaic terms one should more honestly call lust. Don't let yourself be fooled by lust, for lust is not something that lasts, and once it has passed you don't want to find yourself weighed down under all the tediously less transient superstructure of commitment. I've warned my young niece on that score; I told her plain, if a boy insists he loves you, don't believe him; when he says that, all he's doing, all he's really telling you is that he wants to put his penis inside you. Hopefully she'll lead a more guarded teenage knowing that.

So, ever so cautiously, I had to introduce Rula to the thought of returning to work. Rather weirdly, I was a little concerned in particular about that because of her astonishing improvements with spoken English. At last, she'd fully grasped the need to include the definite and indefinite article in a sentence, and with that understanding plus a new and very passable English accent she was a changed woman. I don't know how she'd managed it so quickly, perhaps it was from being away from Magda, as when in private together they always conversed in their own language. Could it be she had learned by listening to me? Was that really possible when she'd had my exclusive company for only a couple of weeks? I mean, I remember how I'd once had the misfortune of working for a period in Birmingham, it was a major software roll-out for a big corporate; yet after three months in that dismal place, sitting alongside a team of brummies, I didn't find myself speaking as if I had a cleft palate and overlarge adenoids. So just a couple of weeks—that was some going, she must have a natural gift for languages. Anyway, what concerned me about it was that her regular clients might not find her so desirable now, not with the absence of her somewhat intriguing foreign accent to excite their encounters. I must say it had turned me on when I first knew her; I found it very alluring. The change in her wouldn't stop desperate men coming to her to turn a trick, I knew that, but it might have a negative impact on her reputation, and there were plenty of other foreign whores working locally who already provided competition to Benny's side-line.

I didn't mention my thoughts to her. Maybe I was just worrying about my own business interest in the flats above the burger bars, and sharing my concern would have appeared grubby.

"Won't you miss me?" she wheedled. "We are so good together."

"Of course I will," I answered, and meant it. "But I shall see you again soon, at Benny's. You need to get back on your own two feet," I added, "you don't want the ignominy of becoming a kept woman."

"But I won't be on my feet for much of the time," she pointed out archly. "You don't mind?"

It was her choice what she did for a living. Better than trimming cod at the city's fish dock. Why should I mind? I smiled and shook my head.

She took my car, to avoid being spotted by any roaming McAllister with the description of a blue Porsche in his mind's eye, and I promised to call in by the weekend.

"I'll miss Sniffer," she called, driving off.

That was a month past. There have been no visits from anyone from the McAllister clan. I routinely have few callers. There had been the postie in his orange jacket and ridiculous shorts that he wears all year round, braving Sniffer's fierce reception from time to time, and one day recently a man in a suit called to enquire whether I might consider voting Conservative in the forthcoming local election. I hadn't even realised there was an election due, and I told him to bugger off; I'd never forgiven them for Brexit.

Then, this morning, a knock at the front door had me standing on the doormat with my gun behind my back, looking Alan Mackie in the face.

"Long time no see," he began. God, how I deplore these platitudinous clichés.

"Sooner than I had anticipated," was my rejoinder.

"How are you—and Rula?" he enquired. "I was looking out for your airborne warrior just now."

"I am well and, as for Rula, I'll pass on your enquiry when I see her next."

He looked disappointed. "Oh, I see you're in an obtuse mood this morning, shall I go away?"

Having been rumbled, my resistance crumbled and I beckoned him indoors. One of the postie's visits had been to deliver a new guitar and I was keen to show it to Alan.

"Mmmm," he murmured disapprovingly, sniffing, "it's a Fender." But it was irresistible, no ordinary Fender in its pink paisley finish, and he grabbed it, saying, "But I can always fancy a nice shiny Acoustasonic Telecaster—limited edition too. Very Sixties."

So we sat for half an hour whilst he ran through some old blues favourites, and I kept his mug filled with fresh coffee. It seemed he had overcome his prejudice towards the brand and, once I had nailed his style, I plugged in my Precision Bass, and together we ran through a noisy rendition of the old Robert Johnson number, Crossroads. That's the virtue of a detached house, no neighbours to bang on the wall.

"What brings you to my door," I asked him eventually, as I wiped down the guitar with a soft cloth. I can't bear finger-marks spoiling the pristine shine. "Are you still up at Knock Hall?"

"Came from there today," he confirmed. "My first day out. Look!" He took a turn up and down my hall. "No limp. Her medic friend worked wonders."

"Good for him," I agreed. "And you, of course."

"Evangeline asked me to bring you a message," explained Alan, "that's what brought me to your door. I have some news of my own for you too."

"Good news, I hope." I was wondering what it meant that he'd used her forename.

"News is news," he quipped.

"Don't tell me the two of you are going to be married." That would have been a blow for the inheritance.

He laughed and laughed at that. "Are you mad?" he shrieked. "She may have unusual poise for an old woman but she's still heterosexual. No, Evangeline's news that I bring you is that she's moving out of Knock Hall. The incident with Ronnie McAllister seems to have really knocked her off balance, she's never quite recovered her sangfroid. She feels vulnerable in that house, and sitting on top of enough weaponry to prosecute a war in the Balkans makes her doubly nervous, what with the Saltire's impending mobilisation too. Sadly, it was always a problem, but I have observed she's drinking much more heavily these days."

I thought of the confidently haughty and upright woman in her dungarees and green wellies who had intervened to help out with the dognappers. My, how a proud mind can be turned to jelly.

"So, is she going abroad?" It seemed unlikely for such a local fixture, but she could afford it, to get away from the Scottish winters in her old age.

"No, she has some land she's going to develop and move on to."

Across the Avenue from her house and all the way down to the crossroads, there's a rather delightful meadow, full of a succession of wild flowers through the year, watered by a natural spring, and with a small fir wood at the top end that has long provided a calming cut-through on my walks around the Knockhall area with Sniffer. Deer seek refuge there in the long grass and cow parsley, and it's where Sniffer often turns up a pheasant. That the meadow comprised an element of the Knock Hall estate I had never known until Alan told me, and the Duchess proposed to build herself a house upon it.

I had mixed feelings when Alan explained her proposal. I regretted the thought that this quiet spot would be destroyed; I also recognised that this land was a part of an estate I expected to inherit, and felt dismayed by what was happening to something that was almost mine, without there having been any discussion.

"She's set on it," said Alan. "The fir trees have already been sold to a timber merchant and will come down next week. It seems she received outline planning permission some time ago and has been sitting on the project."

He could see I wasn't especially excited by her plan.

"Of course," he continued, "this means things are going to change for you."

"They are?" Yes, my pastoral rambles up to the castle would be less enjoyable.

"Of course," he confirmed. "Evangeline will no longer be *in situ* at the house to watch over our merchandise. You'll have to take over that obligation. After all, you already share responsibility as the son of our original trustee. We are counting on it."

I'd already wondered if this was where he was leading me.

"So," he resumed, "you can move in and get your inheritance early."

Well, sort of. It would only be a state of transition until the Duchess carked it, although that surely couldn't be a long way off by the look of her, especially if she'd gone all flaky. I admit I wasn't wholly displeased by the prospect of becoming laird of the manor, so to speak, but I didn't like the thought that the Duchess had discussed my inheritance with Alan.

"How long?" I asked. "The build will take months, of course."

"Not too many months," he answered. "These kit houses go up in no time."

"But moving just a half mile, how does that stop her being vulnerable to the McAllister menace? The walls of a modern house typically offer less security than her current granite dwelling."

"Don't you bet on it," he laughed. "This new house will have all the tech she needs to live a safe, secure and luxurious lifestyle." Alan gave a rueful smile. "And I suppose we will have paid for it; the Saltire, I mean."

That significant conversation took place six weeks ago, if you're trying to keep track of the sequence of events I'm sharing with you. After a fortnight, I'd resumed regular walks around Knockhall with Sniffer, going up the Avenue to the castle ruins and back down the old farm road, always on the look-out for dodgy characters—in particular, anyone in a flashy yellow car. The Duchess's contractors had moved at a pace, and after three weeks of shifting earth from here to there and back again, including the excavation of a deep pit that I assumed was for a wine cellar, they had levelled a sizeable plot with hardcore and were laying pipework, a power supply and foundations. I never called in at the Hall on these walks,

I sensed she wouldn't welcome a fresh reminder of that day in the tunnel, but I always took a peek in the garden as I passed her drive, just to check there were no n'er-do-wells hanging about. All I saw that was out of the ordinary was a huddle of large military-looking tents pitched on her lawn; it all looked very tidy. Alan's North East Chapter presumably. I didn't care to look closer.

Now after six weeks of exceptional industry (I guessed they were being paid well), builders were already erecting the frame for the house. By the broad footprint marked out on the ground, it looked as though it was going to be a huge dwelling.

After two months, my guess was vindicated early one evening. Where once we'd been accustomed to saunter through a peaceful boulevard of firs between the avenue and the farm road, now stood a brazenly large house whose ostentatious credentials seemed to smite with their glare what was left of the trees that lined the meadow. Such incongruity was almost painful to behold. It appeared to be one of those five or six bedroom, three bathroom, custom-designed homes the like of which one sees built for oil executives down on Deeside. A two storey and asymmetric gable window stared down the length of the meadow to the crossroads, like an eye with a dropped eyelid, daring anyone to approach unseen and uninvited. (Which I did, to examine the mystifying annexe that was attached to the house; it contained nothing baffling after all, just a deep pit that was probably going to be a swimming pool.) To me, the whole triple-glazed, wood-panelled edifice appeared crass, a swelling example of conspicuous consumption. The asymmetry of the huge window was an obvious design error. I only assuaged my ill feelings towards this house with the thought that one day it would be mine, and there were plenty of cash-rich fools in the vicinity who'd pay big money to take it from me.

So this was how the Duchess had decided to spend her ill-gotten gains; and all I'd bought was a new guitar!

In the days that followed, there was much activity outside, with landscaping around the new house turning the natural slope of the meadow into terraces and patios, including arbours for seating and tiled paths made to step through a new lawn; and not only landscaping but the installation of intruder alarms, cameras and lights for the house, the entire plot finally girdled by bright steel fencing that was topped with razor wire, and with electronic gates erected at the farm road exit. I speculated whether the razor wire was legal, but I think I have already mentioned that Mrs Delacroix was thought to have powerful connections. Anyway, quite a fortress, it seemed to me.

But I have been so engrossed by telling you about this local development—probably a sign of my irritation—that I never got round to relating Alan's own news, six weeks old now, and much has happened meantime, which I shall relate shortly when my nerves have been restored. To continue: once Alan had delivered the Duchess's intel he had an interesting morsel of his own that later proved to have some real consequences for me, hence my reference to frayed nerves.

Men from the North East Chapter of the Saltire had indeed spent a fortnight at Knock Hall, pitching tents on the Duchess's front lawn as I'd observed, and practising stealth tactics in the long grass of the meadow across the Avenue. I know I would have laughed if I'd seen them, grown men slinking on knees and elbows through the undergrowth with guns in their hands, just as my brother and I had done when playing war games as boys. Only, this was no game, as Alan made clear from the start of his narrative.

"We'd been preparing for this for a long time," he asserted. "Time to stop all the pretence of being a philanthropic pressure group, time for action at last."

Yet I was none the wiser what form the action was expected to take, and it seemed he too had been kept as much in the dark as me in terms of detailed plans. All he could say was that he had been instructed to prepare his men for readiness. It sounded horribly but vaguely portentous. But I can impart what detail he was able to tell me, which was both risible and exciting at the same time. Risible, I suppose, because I have a natural contempt for the political machinations of my fellow man, most of which I feel are fired by hubris and which, ultimately, prove unachievable. But exciting, yes, since it appealed to my own love of mischief.

He brought up the topic of the recent local elections where, apparently, his people—presumably Saltire adherents—had managed to gain control of the regional (i.e. Aberdeenshire) council. It seemed no big deal to me, this was the organisation that dealt with waste collections, presided over planning applications and kept the roads clear of snow in winter. How was taking control of a regional administration such a coup? I know political parties like to own councils in order to progress national policies, but the Saltire wasn't a political party—was it?

So, what had this takeover to do with the Saltire's cloak-and-dagger strategy, surely he knew enough to explain that. And explain it he did, although it was all rather opaque to me still. According to Alan, it cleared the table for, as he so authentically put it, a whole new menu to be served. What the

129

Saltire had in mind now would have any formal wheels oiled that were necessary to its success. Bureaucratic and other official barriers could be leapt, lowered or simply ignored. Evangeline, he said, and there was that first name use again, Evangeline had been very useful in reassuring non-Saltire councillors of our best intentions. She was well-known and well respected as a local upholder of all things decent in establishment minds. Tempting them to dinners at Knock Hall had, over a long period, proved invaluable in winning them over. Local venison had been served (please—not deer from my meadow!) and fine brandy quaffed. I could guess where the brandy had come from to oil those wheels.

"So, you knew Mrs Delacroix before we visited together?" I was feeling a little like the odd man out.

"Oh, yes, Evangeline and I go way back. She's been a committed agent of the Saltire programme since before I became a devotee. It was her idea that I attend those dinners to give talks about the Saltire's aims and objectives—a spot of PR to reassure everyone, to raise enthusiasm for the changes we are pursuing."

There you go, didn't I say one can never know what's going on in the mind of a woman? I shared my gripe with Alan, but he just shrugged and said it is the same with everyone, woman or man, unless you are gifted with extra-sensory perception. I suppose he was right and I should be less gender intolerant. She was under no obligation to tell me anyway. We barely knew each other.

It was at the Duchess's invitation that Alan could bring the North East Chapter to Knock Hall for exercises.

"We pitched our big dorm tents on her lawn," he crowed; "the lads loved it, being out in the fresh air with lovely views across the wildlife sanctuary over the river. Food cooked on her enormous barbecue, taking pot-shots at rabbits in the soft evening light, it was a fun camping trip for most of them. Except during the day—I worked them hard: running, weight and obstacle training, weapons disassembly and reassembly, and sessions discussing political theory. That last was probably the most demanding, at their peak they're not a terribly cerebral bunch."

"So, you said you were preparing them for something, are they now suitably prepared for it, whatever 'it' might be?" It had all sounded horribly like a cocktail of boy scout antics and an episode from the Hitler youth. It certainly smelled alarmingly military.

"We're prepared for anything," he laughed, and there was a menace in his tone that I had not heard since he'd threatened Ronnie's stepson.

I shook my head to clear my thoughts. "You surely know what's going to happen next, even if you haven't been given the details?"

He had taken a while to answer, and he began with a question. "What do you think of our present government," he asked, "specifically the prime minister?"

I had no hesitation in unloading the contempt I carried with me towards that mendacious and corrupt body, particularly the despite with which I held the man who occupied the role of leader. Perhaps it was incautious of me to speak with scant restraint, but I had a strong sense of where Alan was coming from.

"Mmmm," he muttered, digesting my outburst, "well you won't be thrilled to know that the PM is to visit these parts in a week or two. He rarely comes to Scotland, he knows what

131

folk here think of him, but having been rattled by the local election results north of the border he's trying to show that the Union is strong. We didn't take control only of Aberdeenshire, you know, and I think he's been stung. His mini-tour of selected safe sites is to be topped off by a rally up in Moray, whose council is also ours now, at Baxter's of Speyside I understand. You'll know that they are his supporters, of course."

"And...?" I'd guessed what was coming.

"We'll be there."

"We—in what capacity?"

"A welcome party, naturally." Alan's grin was broad and mocking. "Want to join us? It should be fun."

I immediately thought of his declaration that the North East Chapter men had been prepared for some kind of action and I imagined the worst. Alan saw the look on my face and laughed, not unkindly.

"Think about it," he said. "There's time. It will be a nice day out, and you shouldn't be in danger of seeing any of McAllister's people up there, which will be a relief for you. I don't suspect they're fans of political virtue signalling, which is what we can expect to hear."

I still hadn't answered him when he winced and cursed to himself: "Damn, I meant to tell you; you know when we were all camped around her house, me and my men, well there were a couple of incidents. The first was no big deal, really, but it was dramatic to see—a sizeable sinkhole appeared downhill of the house towards the river. That tunnel I imagine; too far down the slope to worry us, if you know what I mean, but that confirms it, there's certainly no access from the far end anymore."

"The second I didn't see, but some of the lads reported finding two oiks sniffing around their tents one evening as they came back from a run. Obvious villains, they said, pretending they were here from the health department, checking we weren't breaking any safety rules, but one of my guys said he kind of knew one of them, a bloke who pretends to be homeless and hungry, sits outside the bank in Union Street with a cardboard placard, begging, is always collected to be driven home in the evening. One of the others who saw him reckoned they knew him to be a dealer, he hangs about the clubs apparently. Anyway, I suspect it was someone looking for information regarding someone else's stepfather, don't you think? You don't normally get people wandering around there now the pikeys have moved on to Peterhead."

This was bad news.

"All the same, they went away empty-handed. Maybe they'll stay away."

"Thank you, Alan." I'm not sure how thankful I really felt to hear about that. "I'll let you know about the Baxters' trip if you can give me your number."

There was another number I had to call—Rula's. If trouble was brewing from the McAllister camp, I had to know if she'd been bothered by them.

She came right away that evening, returning my car but with no news of being approached by anyone with ill intent. Tony had been chaperoning her, accompanying clients to her apartment door and waiting outside until he could hear all was well. I'd have to remember to ask Benny to raise his pay.

Rula appeared not to be harbouring any ill will towards me for not reciprocating her declaration of love and seemed eager to resume our easy-going camaraderie. I didn't actually understand what was going on in her head, but I was grateful not to feel under any more pressure. Over dinner I told her about Alan's visit and his invitation for me to join the Speyside excursion.

"I'm certain there will be trouble," I admitted to her. "And anyway, I'm not really keen on becoming involved in politics, for that after all is what the Saltire are, a political movement, and one with a paramilitary wing."

My contempt for politics was at least equal to my disapproval of all things military, so here I was doubly at far remove from Alan's current venture.

"Politics, it's a complete futility," I told Rula, her eyes wide at the vehemence of my condemnation. "We get one life and when we're gone we're gone. What's the point of wasting your years pursuing political ambition and power when it can never be truly realised, not indelibly anyway. Think of Marxist-Leninism and the USSR, fascism and the Third Reich, social democracy in twentieth-century Britain—all gone, transient. All that striving, all that conflict—pointless. It's all short-termism. And the corruption, the falsehoods, all that seems to be a requirement of being a politician."

She was nodding, but I could tell she wasn't entirely in agreement.

"In my country, it is the same," she said. "Men there achieve power through the use of their wealth, their connections, their willingness to steal, just so that they can be more wealthy and more powerful. That's what we know as politics back home. If there is an ideology, it is a pretence."

It sounded familiar. Yet Rula wasn't finished.

"But you have to take part, you can't stand aside, you have to do what you can to improve things for ordinary people, you have to fight back even if that means doing it under the banner of a political creed. Your adopted political dogma will never persist, but you might do some lasting good along the way."

Wow, I'd never seen this side of Rula. Despite the corruption in her own country, the pedagogy in her schooling must have been inspired.

She sat looking at me for a long moment, then a smile spread over her face. "I know you're a bit of an old cynic," she said, "but I think you always like to do the right thing. Why not go along with Alan, hear what this charlatan the prime minister has to say and then take the opportunity to challenge him on it?"

I didn't imagine we'd have a chance of getting close enough for me to engage the PM in debate, but I had been roused by Rula's sincere sentiments about the imperative to do good and fight back against the elite. I hadn't admitted it to myself before then, but I was also rather intrigued to find out what Alan was planning to do. It was that lure of adventure again—it stays with you. If I found myself, a part of something that might help sweep away the toxic hegemony at Westminster, I was up for it, whether I was a misanthrope or not. So as not to overthink the matter I called Alan before we went to bed. He sounded pleased at my decision, and he promised to drop me some Saltire leaflets in the post, so that I could understand from a more informed standpoint what they were all about.

Of course, us both having been drinking and unable to drive, Rula had to stay the night. Over the past month I'd called in to Benny's to see her, but this was the first time we'd had a chance to enjoy a fuck together, and I was relieved from the pillow talk not to hear mention any more of her inclination towards permanence in our arrangement. I did, however, have to let her share my toothbrush.

10

The leaflets that Alan sent me at first made me laugh, my old scepticism towards political manifestos kicking in. The Saltire was indeed a political organisation, I was sure of that now, although this characterisation remained opaque on their official website. Despite my distrust of political declarations, some of the material did engage my interest.

For a start, they made it clear that their end-game was an independent Scotland, an aim with which I had always sympathised anyway, and a whole booklet of facts and figures was deployed to demonstrate how Scotland was the economic loser in the so-called partnership of the Union.

I was easily convinced, I was aware of that, given my feelings already towards the Westminster government. But the factual arguments did all ring true for me, so much so that even the more emotive arguments concerning the disparagement of Scottish culture, our exclusion from nation-wide decisions on strategic matters, and contempt for environmental and humanitarian concerns north of the border, all this and more I was able to consider rationally and without my usual dismissal of doctrinal submissions as bunk.

Alan called me the night before the excursion to Speyside.

"Are you with us?" he enquired.

"Yes," I answered, "I'm still planning to come with you tomorrow."

"No, are you with us?" There was mischief in his emphasis.

As galvanised by the literature as I was, I was unable to give him the commitment he sought. I wanted first to see just how the Saltire was going to go about matters, and I told him so. He didn't press me any further. "You'll see, I can promise you that," he rang off with a laugh.

We were away early in a white Range Rover on a road silky with frost. I was in the first of three vehicles, sitting next to the driver, a taciturn young fellow with arms so densely tattooed I thought he was wearing an undershirt. Alan introduced him as Murdo. An early bird catches the worm, was how Alan justified the early start, and in this case the worm was known to vary his timetable in order to confuse potential protest groups.

When we reached, it the A96 was fairly quiet which, it being late in the year was not unexpected, but after passing through Fochabers we came upon our first demonstration. The SNP crowd, explained Alan, pointing, they had taken over the last roundabout before the Baxter's venue, their presence a storm of waving saltire banners and crudely drawn placards, the most polite of which called for the PM to go back home.

The sight of all those blue flags brought to mind a question that had been itching to get out. "Isn't there a risk you will be confused with them?" I asked Alan. "I mean, they claim the saltire as their national insignia, and you have that for your organisation's name."

He shook his head. "No way. There's a distinct difference." And when I raised my eyebrows to draw him out further, he explained, "It's the difference between talking and doing, and doing is what we are all about today."

A small gathering in Baxter's car park had assembled before our arrival. The party faithful, I assumed. With our three Range Rovers parked up amongst their Bentleys, Jags and other, newer Range Rovers, we looked inconspicuously part of the sycophantic melee. It was another reason we stayed in our vehicles, all one dozen of us.

A podium had been set up to the side of the Baxter's entrance and a man in a grey suit stood in front of it, talking on a two-way radio and looking down the drive expectantly. It seemed we had arrived in time. Another two suits were standing at the turn-in from the road and Alan informed me they'd be Special Branch. "If you're lucky, they'll take your picture," he told me, "you'll be famous—in certain circles."

The idea didn't appeal.

"If it happens, don't try to stop them," he warned. "Not if you don't want to be arrested as a vagrant or person of interest, or whatever they use as an excuse these days. He indicated with a nod the group of uniformed police who were hanging about at the beginning of the driveway. I saw there was also a couple from Scottish Television, a reporter with one of those microphones clad with a woolly muffle and a cameraman lugging a chunky camera on his shoulder."

And then the pantomime began with the arrival of a large black limousine and murmurs from the party faithful. In fact, not one but two limousines, with our target visible in the back of the second car. It was covered in broken eggs and great dobs of that horrible green slime that kids so love to play with. The SNP contingent that had thrown it were following it along the road and they were chanting and booing for all they were worth. I was already enjoying myself. The television duo seemed to be chortling too.

It was at this point, as the two black vehicles pulled up in front of the party faithful, who surged forward with excitement, that the eleven Saltire men and I quietly exited our vehicles, Alan dragging a holdall out from under his seat. From it, he retrieved a shiny black globe that I at first thought was a helmet. Well, that made sense to me, and I didn't think of it as significant; demonstrators often wear motorcycle helmets for protection against police brutality.

But instantly he disabused me by turning the globe in his hands so that I could read the word BOMB stencilled in large white letters on the side, as well as notice the yellow fuse poking from a slit in the top. It was exactly like those images of a bomb that were drawn for the kids' comics of my childhood; cartoon villains would use them to blast their way into a bank. "Here," he said, handing me the bag, "you take this. And don't let go of it for chrissake." The emptied bag still felt weighty, but I had no chance to look inside as our group pressed forward to mingle invisibly with the PM's cheering cronies.

The PM was still sat in his car while the uniformed plods turned their attention to keeping back the shrill advances of the SNP, and the two Special Branch sleuths took to surveying the party faithful for anything out of the ordinary. Other than Murdo's tattoos, now hidden under his jacket sleeves, we were all twelve of us the model of ordinary in our sober suits. (I had bought mine for my father's funeral and it was very sober.) We blended perfectly with the PM's supporters, only there were no longer twelve of us standing together, for out of the corner of my eye I saw Alan walking calmly and steadily

140

towards the PM's egg-spattered car where the man's bodyguard stood waiting for the all-clear behind an open rear door.

Alan had reached the car before anyone cried out. It was in fact the PM's bodyguard, who leapt forward from the vehicle with a shout, but not quickly enough to stop Alan placing the bomb on the bonnet of the car. I saw STV's cameraman focusing his device onto the bomb and felt sure that the word BOMB would be clearly visible on this evening's news broadcast. Certainly the sight of it stopped the bodyguard in his tracks; long enough, that was, for Alan to flick open his cigarette lighter and touch the fuse, before running off down the drive to cheers from the SNP, who busied themselves tripping up those cops who made to give chase. The last I saw of Alan he had jumped onto the back of a motorcycle that seemed to appear from nowhere and he was gone from sight in a flash.

Meanwhile, with great urgency and frustration, the bodyguard was dragging the flabby corpulence of our national leader from the back seat of the limousine. Amidst screams and cries of dismay from the party faithful, they both fell in a heap onto the ground just as the bomb erupted—not in a terrible explosion, but with a shower of variegated stars and crackling effervescence. The party faithful immediately went from screams of fear to shrieks of delight as the giant firework filled the afternoon with its delightful display. The PM, dusting himself down, tried a smile and nodded at his supporters, as if it were he were the pyrotechnician who had arranged the stunt, but I could see he was shaken and managing to walk only with the support of the bodyguard, with one of the Special Branch men in close attendance.

Nonetheless, the speaking event wasn't abandoned. After a swig from a plastic cup, the PM mounted the podium and began his usual diatribe against Remainers, socialists, anti-Unionists and other ingrates who didn't share his vision of—what, I didn't quite catch it. I heard him spout the word strategy, his strategy, and felt myself groaning, it was all broken record stuff—the crook has never had a strategy other than self-aggrandisement.

We'd managed to insinuate right to the front of the small crowd, and I was amazed to find myself so close to the PM that I could see the rivulets of sweat on his cheeks, and the unmistakeable look of fear in his piggy eyes. He'd obviously been soundly rattled by Alan's extravagant firework.

I became aware of Murdo standing next to me. "Look at him," he snarled. "Cunt!" Murdo lowered his voice when the woman in a bright ruby hat who stood next to us glared with quiet rage.

To cover his expletive I remarked, "How extraordinarily close to the PM we've been allowed to stand. Whose idea of security has allowed this morning's shambles?" It was as useless and chaotic as practically everything else this administration turns its hand to, but the woman in the hat nodded in grim endorsement.

Murdo's explanation was delivered in a hiss: "He likes to think he's everybody's pal, no-one wants to hurt him, but I dare say he has no friends other than the ones he buys with gifts and preferment."

"Yes," that was nothing new, "but consider," I said to him, "this situation would present quite an opportunity for somebody seriously meaning to do him harm."

"Smile for the camera," he answered, for Special Branch were taking pictures of us all. They moved down the line in front of the PM, who was still waffling, and Murdo shook my arm, out of the side of his mouth urging, "Come on, then, what's keeping you? You be serious and stop posing for the camera." He rolled his eyes towards the pair from Special Branch, who now had their backs to us. "Come on," he said again, shaking the holdall whose handles I was gripping tightly, "you're the man with the gun. Finish the fucker before he makes me throw up with his bullshit."

At last, I opened the holdall to discover the weight inside belonged to Alan's long-barrelled revolver. It was like finding a deadly snake coiled inside an innocently folded garment. In my shock at the sight of it, and thinking rapidly of all the ramifications of being there in possession of a lethal weapon, I totally lost my equilibrium. Folk were jostling, trying to shuffle closer to their leader, and my own proximity to him was ebbing, so that quicker than you might imagine, I was losing my line of sight. If I fired now, I'd probably blow the head off the shoulders of the woman in the ruby hat, who'd pushed in front with her phone held aloft, no doubt hoping for a selfie with the PM.

I found myself dissembling to cover my hesitation. Don't get me wrong, I have no difficulty with the idea of a dishonourable politician being disposed of, and I'd often wondered, could I erase a man just because his ideas were abhorrent to me? But what ate at me most just then was that this was not the place for murder. Here in the sunshine of Moray, a quiet coastal settlement where dolphins frolic in the waves offshore, and where the gold of the barley harvest was being turned into first-rate single malt—liquid gold, if you ask me, in more ways than one. It just didn't gel.

Here was a place I'd felt welcomed on previous visits, and I think I was refusing to spoil the memories. You may well charge that I was smothering my inaction with spurious thoughts, that I was spinning words like an indulged TV academic, but to my mind in that particular frozen moment it would have been close to sacrilegious to slaughter a man amongst such an agreeable environment. Wouldn't it? Don't you agree?

Actually, I don't give a damn whether or not you do, but a storm of disconnected thoughts in my head was truly creating havoc out of familiar associations, a confusion that removed me from normal rational judgement. What the French might dismiss as *en passant, une crise de nerfs*, or a barrister would claim as the excuse of temporary insanity. So that's all it was. Okay, I can go along with that.

I recalled towards the end of that long moment of hesitation Rula's edict, that one has to fight these people, the oppressors. But did I care enough? Shooting the dog snatcher had been personal, but this, this would be a cold-blooded assassination. I rationalised my predicament as like to a sexual encounter, where one has to be sufficiently aroused in order to perform well, and I just wasn't fired up at all. Clutched in my hand, inside the holdall, Alan's revolver was the handgun equivalent of a limp dick, and I wasn't in a mood to jerk it off.

There, I'd prevaricated for far too long, or long enough if you think about it another way. The PM had finished his vacuous blether, the sycophants were clapping, Mrs Ruby Hat was beaming, having secured her selfie, and the man at the centre of attention was stepping down, to be escorted by his bodyguard through the doors into Baxter's to enjoy some restorative refreshment.

Coming out of my paralysis, immediately I began to ask myself what had that been all about? Why bring a dozen Saltire men all the way up to the Moray coast for them to do nothing but masquerade as the party faithful and be witness to a firework display? As for myself, I felt useless, a complete wimp, a dupe. But was such excoriation justified? Shouldn't Alan have prepared me for the task instead of just leaving me the weapon? He'd obviously made assumptions about me that were very much wanting. Then there was Murdo, clearly he'd known what was expected; perhaps he thought I'd been briefed. He'd quickly moved away from my disgrace and was standing with two others from our group, sending me sharp glances of disparagement.

I wandered away a little, down the drive, feeling totally disorientated. The two from STV came up to me, the fluffy microphone shoved in my face. "Well, what did you think of that?" the reporter asked.

"What, the firework display?" I replied.

"The speech by Big Dog. Didn't it shine a light for Scotland."

In my befuddled state of mind, the nickname threw me for an instant until I remembered it was the PM's handle amongst his closest cronies. "His speech? It was shit. Totally flatulent. He hates the troublesome Scots. The whole of today's event has been a sham, a heap of crap."

Of course I wasn't thinking about the speech on its own, but I don't imagine my petulant opinion would be broadcast on teatime news anyway.

I sat in the back for the return journey, as far away from Murdo as I could manage. There was little conversation. I huddled inside a bitter feeling of having been unfairly used. I just shouldn't ever get involved with other people's affairs; it always comes out badly. I knew that. It had long been my guiding philosophy and in a moment of weakness I'd wandered from it to my cost.

We stopped in a layby just north of Huntly, where a rough flint track led off into a woodland walk. My mind was immediately sent racing, this was just the place for an execution. Would I be able to make a run for the trees? Then the passenger door was pulled open, and I shrank back. But instead of hands reaching in to haul me out I saw Alan's face, and he squeezed in next to me with no obvious resentment showing in his nod of greeting. With relief, I felt the Range Rover speed away once more.

"A good day, eh?" Alan nudged me. "Scared the shit out of the lot of them. How about you—how did you get on?"

He saw my shamefaced expression. "Didn't score then. I didn't think you would."

"Wh…what do you mean?"

"No discipline. I knew that when I first met you."

"You did?"

"Well, you told me afterwards that you were expecting a visit from someone who was likely to do you harm. You had a gun in your hand for protection. If you'd also had discipline, I wouldn't be here with you now. You didn't know me from any of McAllister's thugs. With discipline, you'd have blown my head off instead of dropping your weapon."

He was insulting me, and I didn't care for it, especially after his trick with the revolver in the holdall.

"I have fired a gun before."

"You don't say so."

"Well, there was a dognapper—"

"Emotion—he was after your dog."

"And then, surely you recall, Ronnie McAllister."

"Same again. Revenge for what he'd done to Rula. No, what I wanted to see was whether you could whack somebody in cold blood. It takes guts, and discipline. It was a test."

"You were testing me?" Bloody liberty.

"I have plans for you, my son. Here, Murdo—" he tapped the driver on the shoulder and slapped a wad of banknotes into his hand. "You won."

"We had a little wager on you," he said to me. "I hope you're pleased I was rooting for you. Anyway," he didn't wait for my reply, "anyway, it was a successful day, we managed to show how poor is the PM's security away from London, and we made him shit his pants in fear."

"Won't that just mean he'll improve his security arrangements?"

"He never improves nothing. No, it just means he'll keep away from where a visit is too risky, it's always that way. And he's been reminded today what we think of him in these parts."

"So will the viewing public."

"Eh?"

"Didn't you see the STV crew?"

"Oh, magic!"

"But, I have to ask, why take a dozen men all that way just so they could mingle with his fans?"

"Is that what you thought? For God's sake! That was my security. If my little enterprise had gone pear-shaped, they'd have caused a major distraction so's I could get away. That was why."

Alan was highly pleased with himself, his cheeks glowed, and I couldn't help admiring the free-spirited image he presented. He saw me looking at the ugly scar on his cheek.

"One can do a great deal of damage with a bottle, my friend." He stared at me for a while. Was that a threat?

I couldn't wait to get home to Sniffer and take him for a long quiet walk on the beach. My emotions were a pent up maelstrom of anger, disappointment and shame, I didn't know which feeling was the strongest. I was also exceedingly irritated to think this daring individual had had the audacity to make plans for me; I wasn't one of his men. And, too, that I'd been demeaned by a wager with our driver. I just couldn't talk any more, that was the safest way to be. I didn't belong with these people, and I longed to be away from them. Just me and Sniffer on our own together, that's how it's best.

11

I did a lot of walking after that black day, trying to bury my sense of shame and at the same time vent my spleen towards Alan. It became a kind of routine, every other day or so going up around Knock Hall to check on the progress with the hated new building, although I avoided paying visits to the Duchess. I'd spy her sometime, over in her vast garden, riding on a mower despite the lateness of the season, or wielding a chainsaw to cut down dead branches that might come crashing with the winter gales. She rather amazed me, a woman of an almost antique countenance but with the fortitude of a younger man. Eccentrically, it seemed she'd taken to wearing tight black leather rather than her customary dungarees, and she looked more like a figure from Washington Irving's 'Legend of Spooky Hollow' as she whirled around on that machine between the spectral trees fronting her lawn, and less the frumpy lady of the manor.

The meadow, I observed, had been used roughly in the exercises undertaken by Alan's men. The sight of the crushed grass in the expanse below the construction site made my thoughts turn to Alan and I realised I had not heard from him since the Speyside debacle. What on earth was it he was planning for me, I wondered. His comment had nagged at me ever since; he had no right to be interfering in my life.

I took the track around the back of Knockhall Castle one afternoon and watched Sniffer race off through the barley stubble in a hopeless chase after a pheasant that had taken noisy flight. Seeing his frustration at the futility of the chase reminded me of my own enigma and I pulled out my mobile phone. It rang for ages before I heard Alan's voice.

"Hello, old man," he answered, having recognised my number. "Good to hear from you." He sounded roundly buoyant.

"Well," I said, "I hadn't heard from you since…you know, our day trip, and just wondered how matters are progressing."

"Oh," he laughed, "I didn't realise you were expecting me to lay on further adventures just yet. Anyway, I'm not in a position to do much on that score as I'm abroad at the moment, will be for quite a while as it turns out. Training, you see. Libya's not a bad place at this time of year, by the way."

He waited for my surprised silence to pass. "Perhaps in the new year, yes that will be it. In the new year, we can really start motoring. New prospects, new energies, it's all about renewal after all. You'll love it, I promise."

I hadn't a clue what he was talking about but the thought that I wouldn't be troubled for a month or two was welcome. We talked a little about current political events, and joked about what the prime minister might be doing after his fright at Speyside, then Alan had to ring off, muttering something about rocket practice, or at least that's what I thought he said. Reception had deteriorated as I walked down through the avenue and my mind has a habit of inserting words when my hearing lapses.

With the extravagant house nearing completion, I was finding the Knockhall walk less of an attraction, seeing that incongruous mansion set down amongst what had been rural tranquillity, so I tended to choose alternatives for my ramblings with Sniffer.

Rula called to ask if she could bring Magda over. She had told her all about our walk in the dunes and her friend was keen to see for herself. I wasn't really ready for human company but, of course, I agreed; Magda was an interesting and intelligent personality, and who could reject the opportunity of walking out with two highly attractive young women? Indeed, she showed herself to be visibly delighted when I introduced her to a wonderfully deserted beach, the tide far out and the late autumn sun sparkling on silver waves as they curled over the bar at the estuary mouth.

We climbed up through the high dunes that come up against fields with sheep and with the Beachborough golf course in the near distance. There, men pushed their little trolleys across the clipped grass in search of an elusive hole in which to sink a ball.

"How silly they look," laughed Rula, "like they're taking their babies for a ride in their push-chairs." But although I shared her sentiment towards that particular game, I was glad there was a golf course to stand in the way of developers, who would relish covering these green hills with sterile housing estates. The whole area has been under attack since the regional council developed its *Energetica* strategy, which foresees a corridor of housing and business development expanding all the way up the coast from Aberdeen to

Peterhead and beyond. I just wish the council would instead apply more of its energetica to conserving the shape and scale of our village. So it was that I felt thankful for golf enthusiasts, even though I don't share their passion for the game.

Magda was fascinated by Sniffer, trying to follow his fast-paced and winding race through the marram grass as he terrorised the dunes' rabbit population, and in all, despite a squally wind off the North Sea, we had a very enjoyable outing. Walking home, I was feeling content, and looked forward to an evening of clever conversation.

Still, as we arrived home I did experience a brief frisson of anxiety when I saw Rula's blue Porsche sat on my drive, but it quickly passed. There had been no McAllister intrusions either here or at Benny's and both Rula and I had ceased to worry ceaselessly about the criminal family's intentions.

Magda, on the other hand, once we were sat with a drink, definitely had a troubled look on her face. I was relieved when it turned out not to be because of worry on Rula's behalf. She, Magda, desperately needed a change, she confided, life had become so mechanistic, so routine.

"It was exciting, our escape from the east," she said. "Scary but somehow enjoyable at the same time. There was a delicious thrill to it despite the constant fear of being stopped and turned over to the authorities. I need some more of that now, something more than a tedious succession of sad men who can't find satisfaction with their wives or girlfriends, or can't even get a girl of their own."

Rula was nodding. "Yes," she chimed in, "what we do is as boring as being on a production line. But unlike working with colleagues in a factory, our clients don't make much conversation. In they come, looking awkward mostly. We make sure they're clean, then we go through the routine; first suck their dick to get them hard, then lie down while they huff and puff on top of us for a few seconds; and when they've finished, give them a towel and tell them how good it was. It's as routine as peeling onions in a pickling plant, but without the chat."

"That's the easy ones," added Magda. "As you know, there are some who want to dominate and abuse, to play out their macho fantasies, but they are few and far between, thankfully. Some others want to kiss me—yuck!—some want to fuck doggy style, and in undignified fashion I'm down on my knees with my face stuffed into the pillow—so demeaning. And perfunctory."

"I had always entertained the impression that you rather liked your work." I had genuinely believed that. "But you find it…"

"Monotonous, repetitive and wearisome, for the most," they both said as one. "Not forgetting the ones who insist they love you," continued Rula, "goodness, they can be a bore." She looked at me with a frown: "I have taken to my bosom what you think of love. In the case of these foolish men, well—"

"The money's good," admitted Magda, "but money is not why we came to the west."

"No," agreed Rula. "We needed freedom—from poverty, yes, but also freedom to live our lives without the burden of control or interference by the state; to be ourselves; to shed also the necessity of enduring routine and drab employments."

"It's what we want still," insisted Magda. "To be our own masters of what we do, not the managed, not the servant. To

153

live life more light-heartedly, and to enjoy being young as long as we can. That's important. No more sad old men."

"Exactly," confirmed Rula. "As you say, a livelihood doing something with our own generation, or younger perhaps, that would be good, if we could find such a thing; so that we might step lightly on the ground instead of dragging a ball on a chain, if you understand me. That's what we want."

Indeed I did understand her, despite my smile at her rather whimsical expression. Since the episode at Speyside and, I suppose, after the worry of the McAllister threat, not forgetting the unease I'd already felt from secretly laundering my new fortune; since all of that had built up like a waiting avalanche, suspended and ready to spew its blows down through the reaches of my worrying imagination, it had indeed seemed that I was dragging a great weight on a chain behind me.

As I sat with the two girls and listened to them turning over between them a long inventory of possible new futures, which evidently they had been adding to for some time, I began to speculate over fresh options for myself. Not random day dreaming, I assure you, but with some method, and helped by interjections from Rula and Magda once my silence had brought their own discussions to a close.

I had been reasonably content before discovering the three suitcases. Not wealthy but not struggling financially, either. Freelance IT jobbing does more than keep the wolf from the door, and you don't have to give a toss for company culture if you're not a salaried employee. No, it had been what you might call comfortable. I had my dog, whom I valued as my principal companion, I lived in a pleasant location, and I was kept busy with my garden and my studying, methodically filling in all the intellectual gaps left by an inadequate schooling.

The money bonanza hadn't improved on all that. But it had given me a headache that was not there previously. For now, I was going to have to manage an estate I'd never aspired to own, and one with a black poison in its underbelly, an illegal cache of weaponry belonging to what most likely was the next big terrorist threat in Scotland. The Saltire, they were probably my biggest encumbrance; I'd been saddled with a clandestine organisation of which formerly I knew nothing, but which by virtue of my father's business threatened to have a profound and unwelcome influence over my previously untroubled existence.

"That bastard!" I exclaimed, coming out of my absorption.

"Which one?" demanded Magda, looking suddenly discomfited.

"Mackie, Alan Mackie. He's my bête noir at the moment," I conceded.

Of course, after that outburst I had to tell them both the story of my inglorious Speyside adventure and the threat that hung over me in the shape of Alan's opaque plans for next year.

Rula looked quite upset for me and came and sat on my lap to give me a hug. It was nice of her, but it made me feel even more of a wimp. Magda simply shook her head and said, "There's a simple solution to this quandary," and proceeded to tell me in no uncertain terms what I should do. I had already arrived at the same conclusion she presented, a way out for me that would have the added indulgence of payback for what I felt had been my humiliation. I decided to sit on the idea for a while, just to top and tail it, but I promised myself I'd be ready for Alan's return from whatever wrongdoings he'd been perpetrating in north Africa.

The two women had resolved to make a break with their current profession by year end, although they had no idea what they would do next, and they beseeched me to explain their resolve to Benny; they were aware how let-down he would feel, given they had been his side-line's first and longest employees.

So the three of us celebrated our determination for a new future with a fresh bottle of Sancerre, toasting the approach of Christmas and the new year as a time of renewal and fresh opportunity, after which a most generous-spirited Magda proposed that, as her thank-you for an enjoyable afternoon, the two of them should entertain me together, as they had done my father a few Christmases past. Fortunately, the experience didn't deliver the same fatal outcome.

Death, however, hovered close by, one consequence of which was the acceleration of my plans.

With winter weather drawing in, I resumed my regular Knockhall walks, since braving the cold north winds and horizontal rain on the open beach made walking there more of a trial of endurance than a pleasure. Even with the sky firing pellets of ice at my face (the Met Office had forecast it as snow showers), a walk around the castle was less of an ordeal, with the trees on the Avenue and down the farm road providing a modicum of shelter.

On a couple of occasions, I spied the Duchess in her new dwelling, her spidery outline flickering across the huge gable window, and I wondered how it must feel to be alone in that huge place. It lacked the familiar reassurance of the old house with its ancient beeches standing guard along her entrance drive, and the cosy leaded panes of her south-facing windows with their echo of Dickensian cheer. Rather spitefully I speculated on the temperature inside that new building once I spied an air source heat-pump contraption up against her new wall. Still, it had always seemed cold in Knock Hall, so maybe she'd not notice the chill. She once waved on an occasion when she saw me, but I did not take it as an invitation to go in. There were workmen there at the time, at least there were two vans parked near her front door, electrical contractors it appeared from their livery. I chose not to intrude.

The temperature of my life seemed to have reached an equable level over several successive days until, one stormy Saturday afternoon, and with only a couple more days to go to Christmas Eve, Sniffer and I had battled up the Avenue against a biting north-easterly gale, with a hail of twigs and large snowflakes falling about us, and had just taken the track past the castle, when I heard a faint cry from below the hill, seemingly from the new house. Looking down through the scrubby grass, on the western side of the building where the Duchess's new drive came in from the farm road, I could see the postie's bright red van parked just inside the electronic gates, which I assumed the postie had been given the means to open; but the voice that sought help came from nearer the house and I glimpsed through the increasingly heavy snowfall a figure standing in front of the garage, gesticulating excitedly at me. It was the postie, and his attitude was one of extreme agitation.

Because of the grimly effective fencing that encircled the whole development site I had to carry on beyond the castle and back down the farm road before I could gain access to the grounds of the house. Either that or go all the way back to the Avenue where I knew there was a gap in the fence. I took the former route, for the wind would be behind us, and fortunately we found the security gates had been left open, so I ran in with Sniffer where once we had sauntered through a small fir wood.

"Oh thank you, I just saw you passing," cried the postie, his words slashed by the wind. "I can't raise her; this is the third time this week I've tried, and now I've quite a bundle of stuff for her majesty." He showed me a sack he'd put down in the snow. Unceremoniously, he grabbed my arm and dragged me around to the tall south-facing gable window. "And now I'm concerned for the woman, look there—"

He pulled me up close to the window and urged me to peer inside. The room was sparsely furnished, a large sofa taking up much of the wall to the right and a round white table dominating the centre. The floor was bare of coverings; a light wooden floor swept clean owned the space, wall to wall.

"Look," he said again, "look, isn't that curious? She's usually such a tidy woman."

He pointed and on the white table I saw a brandy bottle on its side, presumably empty. There were also some cloths and a stoppered can of something I couldn't make out on the table, plus a small quantity of dark shiny equipment, one piece of which looked like a telescopic sight for a gun. That old uncomfortable chair from the Hall had been pushed back at an angle, as if someone had left in a hurry. So, she'd helped herself to our hoard in the tunnel for a drink to accompany some task or other. My immediate thought. '*Well, why not, there was no-one here to cast a disapproving eye.*' But no, the postie was pointing across the room where, just visible amongst the plump cushions on the sofa, I could make out the butt and magazine of an automatic weapon. So, she'd helped herself to the Saltire's hoard as well, it seemed.

"It's a puzzle, I dinna ken if she's okay," blurted the postie. I looked again, trying to see beyond the open door from the room, but all that came into view was the pristine white of more walls. But Sniffer could see more, apparently, for at that moment we heard his frantic bark from around the east side of the house and we both raced round, sliding on the icy slush that had built up on the grass.

What he'd discovered was guaranteed to excite him, for there, strutting up and down behind a tall, glazed section of wall was a strikingly coloured pheasant, the vivid red, blue and green of its head like a brilliant disguise for a festive masque ball. The other ball invitee that we could see was not looking so resplendent. Mrs Delacroix lay in a twisted pose on the highly polished wooden floor, which in this section of the house had been expensively parqueted, one leg bent at an unnatural angle beneath the opposing thigh, and a huge crimson wound in her neck. There was a further 'wound' in the ceiling above her, where shards of plasterboard hung by threads.

It took us only moments to find out how the pheasant had gained entry, the tell-tale back door to the linked garage was banging open in the wind. Had she let the bird in, or had it simply been seeking shelter and found its own way in? The latter, most likely, the Duchess was not an especial lover of wildlife, belonging to that class of people who seek pleasure from slaughtering deer, foxes and—well, anything sentient they can get in their sights. This version of events we confirmed when we entered the house, first finding her body and confirming she was dead, there having been a considerable loss of blood that would no doubt ruin the parquet, then her abandoned and discharged double barrelled shotgun on the floor next to her head. The floor itself was slick with brandy all the way from the front lounge, some liquid still spilling from a second overturned bottle on the floor. The gun on the sofa looked as though it had been disassembled for cleaning and was not in a state of dangerous readiness.

It did not require an Inspector Morse to work out that the pheasant was a lucky creature. I hoped the police would reach the same conclusion as me, that this was no crime scene. The most unmistakeable chain of events had surely seen Mrs Delacroix startled by the impertinent arrival of the wayward gamebird. Infuriated she'd given chase, was my supposition. Flinging down the broken gun she'd been cleaning onto the sofa as she ran, and snatching up her shotgun, but holding on to her drink in the way that an inebriate might do, and lurching as she went, she finally got close enough for a shot at the pheasant. But she'd slipped on the shiny wet parquet, that seemed most likely, consequently blasting holes in both the hall ceiling and her throat as she fell. It takes skill and experience to master such a weapon, which aptitude I thought I'd seen in action when she despatched the dognapper. But it takes serious intoxication to consider going on an armed pheasant hunt inside a brand new house. And so it was that the day witnessed her downfall rather than the bird's.

Why she was cleaning one of the Saltire's guns I shall never know, but while the postie went to his van to retrieve his mobile I gathered all the pieces and hid them inside the umbrella stand that now stood in her new hall. Perhaps this had all been part of her neuroticism and she fancied protecting herself with a more modern weapon. Anyway, I had to make sure the police did not find it there or they'd start asking questions with potentially enormous consequences.

The postie had called the police and an ambulance, which I thought was excessive. Should one really call an ambulance for dead people? I would have to find out for future reference. He'd left me his name and contact details and driven off, saying the incident couldn't be allowed to spoil the Christmas of other folk on his round who were expecting the delivery of parcels. I puzzled for a while considering whether his reasoning was callous or compassionate, but I never reached a conclusion for, wandering through the house (I know I was uninvited, but I suppose it was okay as it would soon be mine), I realised I'd entered the annexe, where I came upon a double door guarded by a keypad entry system. The Duchess must have left it unlocked, perhaps after retrieving the gun that I'd just hidden, and, of course, I eased open the door to see what secret it was hiding. There were rough concrete steps down and motion-sensitive lighting that picked out a raised floor at the bottom, a kind of broad mesh in a dark rubbery material. The space was not, as I'd first conjectured, a gun store. Two very large grey boxes stood in the centre of the space below me, upon which red and green lights winked. Both were entirely featureless except for the name 'QuantumTech' affixed in cursive red metal script to both machines, and there was a large saltire sticker in a top corner of each of them. Seriously insulated cables spilled out the backs of the machines and went through the mesh floor. On one wall, there was a white cabinet with flickering dials on the front. It had the letters UPS stencilled on its face. To its side and connected to it was a stand of battery racks, I recognised those from a

161

visit to 'Futureworld' in Orlando, whilst a thick cable went from it into the floor. Hmmm, an uninterrupted power supply meant that this was a critical installation for someone, and the saltire stickers led me to conclude who that someone was. There was a constant hum from fans inside the two featureless computers, which I found unsettling, but it was not loud enough to mask the sound of a police siren approaching. At least, I assumed it was a police car, it could have been an ambulance.

My brain was quickly joining up the dots and I shut the double door behind me. If that was Saltire business down there, it would not do to let the police know about it. For it had been the police who'd arrived with such clamour and not an ambulance. I suppose they have few opportunities to play the blues and twos and will turn on the klaxon whenever they can, just to make themselves appear more exciting and authoritative.

Fortunately, the two plods from the car made the same assumption as me, that there had been no foul play, until in the kitchen we found a tub full of empty liquor bottles and the pheasant, which greeted us with its distinctive hoarse crowing, the moment when one of the plods made a crack that there had demonstrably been foul play after all. Fortunately, before he subjected us to any more of his wit, an ambulance arrived to take the body, which answered my earlier question, I suppose; but I was left wondering whether the old bill would employ such levity when attending a major road traffic accident with multiple casualties. I decided yes, it was their way of avoiding sinking into their own trauma.

Everything seemed to be wrapped up so quickly and with a minimum of fuss, I was expecting further questions or a search of the house, but the plods were concerned only with shooing the bird out of the building and getting on their way as they had a Christmas party to return to. All that was left for me to do was round up Sniffer and let Alan know what had happened. Having found the Saltire's secret server installation I was sure he'd want to know.

12

With the main doors to the outside fast closed and not knowing the code to release the locks, the only exit from the house was through the garage, which was lucky for the ambulance men, since as with a corpse on their trolley rather than an injured patient they were free to manoeuvre it less cautiously through the narrow rear door. When at last Sniffer and I stood on the snowy grass, I jammed the door shut with a plug of wood the joiners had discarded, so that I might return and take the more leisurely look around that I was promising myself. The door codes would surely be noted somewhere inside the house, or most likely Alan would know, as going on what I'd found in the basement, this property seemed to be as much a Saltire interest as Mrs Delacroix's last safe abode.

I had some calls to make when I reached home. First was the Edinburgh notary whose address had been embossed in gold at the top of the disposition document. It being a Saturday I had no luck in raising him, so had to wait until Monday when, having introduced myself and explained about the Duchess having passed, he said little more than that he could do nothing until he had a certificate of death, and that matters of inheritance could take a long time to complete. He also needed to ensure there was no competing will. '*Typical*

164

lawyer,' I thought, but I was in no hurry. He did confirm, however, that he was in possession of a signed facsimile of the Knock Hall disposition, and was familiar with the intended arrangement. I was to send him details that would confirm my identity.

My second call, which did prove successful, was to Alan Mackie. He was still overseas and sounded irritated to have been interrupted. There was thumping music in the background and the sound of men's loud voices. When I gave him the news about the Duchess, he seemed remarkably uninterested, just pointing out that I was now 'the guardian', but when I told him that as the incoming owner of her estate I intended, without delay, to put her fancy new house up for sale, his only words in response were "There's a flight on Boxing Day. Do nothing until I'm back." Then he hung up.

So, Christmas had arrived, and I went over to Benny's for a Christmas Eve party after speaking to the notary. He'd invited a number of the girls employed in his side-line and I had to learn their names as if we'd never met, since I was instructed not to refer to them by their familiar flower appellations, this being designated a day away from work.

"It's alright," said Rula, sitting down on my lap, "you can call me Daisy, 'cos I'm always springing back when you cut me down." She gave me a cheeky smile and hugged me close. "Only joking," she insisted, her breath hot in my ear, but I knew she was not.

"So what's new?" asked Benny, coming over with a tall glass of negroni. It was the moment to tell him my news from three days ago, with Magda and Rula hanging onto my hands and upon my every word.

165

"Have you been back to the house?" Rula chirruped, she was visibly tipsy and excited by my news. And when I said it was my intention to go the next day they protested that I couldn't do that on Christmas Day, not unless they could come too and make it a Christmas adventure.

"I'd love to see inside that place," said Rula, "the way you've described it. To see how the wealthy live, I've never been inside such a fancy-sounding place. This house, Benny's, is the most expensive I've seen."

"You could afford this house," said Benny. "My house."

"I'd like something simpler if I was buying," she retorted. "You know, we were brought up, Magda and me, to think that property is theft. Something like that sticks with you."

Well, that remark killed the easy spirit in our little throng and after agreeing to take the two girls with me the next day, I went to replenish my drink and tried to mingle, busying myself in discovering the real names of Rose, Delphina, Marigold, Tulip and the rest, for I am not a natural mingler.

Christmas Day meant dinner midday with my brother and his family, and as we made merry I was able to tell the story of Sniffer and the pheasant, omitting the more gory description of Mrs Delacroix's decease.

"Adventures always happen to you two," said my brother, accusingly, and I had to remind him that he was (eccentrically, I thought) jetting off to Corfu in a day or two, to go sailing around the Ionian islands, which in wintertime could easily mean it was going to be something of a nautical adventure.

"Don't forget to visit Ithaca," I mentioned. "I've reminded them you're coming." He was to run a little errand for me, delivering a parcel of euros to the dog rescue team I supported.

I excused myself after the pudding and brandy butter, it was my usual time to take Sniffer for his afternoon walk, and I never missed it.

Magda and Rula were waiting in Magda's car, so I collected Sniffer and she drove us—with great care, I must say—around Knockhall and up the, by now, very icy Avenue. Of course, we could have taken the farm road and gone through the main entrance gate, which the postie had left unlocked for the police, but going in through the back added to the sense of adventure for the girls. I'd noticed on my Sniffer walks that the contractors had left a gap in the fence palings just opposite the Knock Hall entrance, perhaps to let the Duchess gain easy access from her old home, and we ducked under the coil of razor wire that stretched above us.

"Burglars, we're like burglars," tittered Magda, when we eased open the rear door to the garage. I didn't feel the same way, for soon I would own this place, but remembering what I'd seen in that basement did make me feel a bit like an intruder on someone else's property. Supposing Major Frisk or some other Saltire big-wig were here? I told the girls to hush, there were sophisticated alarms installed and they might be aurally triggered. Dutifully, all conversation ceased, but I hadn't meant to be that draconian; it was all part of making this an adventure, since I knew from the last time I was here that such alarms were unlikely.

Entering the main house I avoided the corridor where the floor was still messy with bloodstains, and we found another way through to the front of the building. Looking out through triple-glazed glass I was relieved to find no cars parked outside, which almost guaranteed we were alone in the house.

"How many bedrooms, how many bedrooms?" Magda wanted to know, and I guessed five or six.

"Let's go and find out," whispered Rula, who'd discovered a lift in the entrance hall.

The only lifts I had ever encountered in a private house were those of an elderly neighbour with mobility problems and that self-assured couple on television, the big bloke with the facial hair and the arty wife who bought and renovated a French chateau together. But we soon came to realise that this was no ordinary private house.

The lift door opened on a first floor landing wide enough for one to park an SUV. A large brass clock swung its pendulum silently from its place on the wall and there was what looked like a huge original James Morrison skyscape hanging next a broad window, providing continuity with the sweep of clouds we could see through the window. There were indeed six bedrooms with doors off the passage from the lift, but just two were furnished as places in which to sleep, the other four having been fitted out as workspaces, with simple wire-management desks and cable ports set in the wooden floor. At the far end of the passage, we came upon a large room that stretched the width of the house, which appeared to be a conference or meeting room, with some tables and wheeled office chairs, a screen rolled to the ceiling, a bank of telephones and blackout curtains. I got the impression its preparation was still incomplete, the furniture was all higgledy-piggledy, although a chilled water dispenser had been installed next a table with a coffee machine, which lent the appearance of active use. Fortunately, we encountered no-one, and I eventually took my hand away from the pocket where I had my gun, though God knows who I'd expected to have to shoot, or why. But the more we saw in the house that we hadn't expected to discover, the more I felt like an intruder and it wasn't long before I was asking Rula and Magda if they'd seen enough. As we came out of the room I looked back and spied a small dark notice fixed above the door, which somehow I'd missed going in. 'Situation Room', it read, and I shuddered at its presumptuousness.

They wanted to go back to the ground floor and I decided I'd have to steer them away from the annexe with its entrance to the server room, I was struggling to remember whether I'd shut the doors properly. As it happened, in guiding them away from the place where Mrs Delacroix had had her fatal accident, we traversed a corridor and came upon those double doors, which to my relief I had closed tight.

"What do you think is in there?" probed Rula, shaking the door handles. "It must be a basement as there's a small stair just behind us that seems to lead to a mezzanine above it, and anyway the doors are too grand for a cupboard."

She went back and climbed the four stairs. "Yes, it's a games room up here. It's in that extension of the main building."

"If this were a castle, it'd be the entrance to a dungeon," laughed Magda, taking hold of the door handles and pulling uselessly.

"Wine cellar most like," I suggested. "She used to like a drink, apparently."

"But why would a wine cellar have a red light over the door?" asked Rula, pointing.

I hadn't noticed it before, a simple red bulb in a socket. It was not lighted and could be easily missed in shadow.

"Perhaps she was running a brothel in there," I laughed, to cover my oversight. "Would you like to have a red light outside your door?"

That brought me looks of severe disapproval from Magda, which I acknowledge was wholly justified, while Rula simply sighed, "Unreconstructed male." But there was no time for acrimony, for at that moment Magda hissed and pointed at the window. The triple glazing must have silenced his approach but there walking up the drive from his car was, speak of the Devil, Major Frisk. Surely he hadn't heard the news of Mrs Delacroix's demise? No, he walked with a jaunty step and was cheerily whistling Colonel Bogie, when I would have expected more reverence from a man of his bearing.

"Time to go," I insisted. "We can come back again when I'm the rightful owner. We can have a grand party to celebrate." I was thinking of that colourful pheasant and how a masque ball would be good. We could hold it in the Situation Room. But glancing at the house as we scrambled through the fence onto the Avenue, I saw the upright figure of Major Frisk crossing the lighted window of that strange large room upstairs, his mobile phone pressed to his ear. Had he seen us depart?

"You know," started Rula, selecting another cannabis cake from the repurposed mince pie box and sipping her tea, "I think that secret place with the red light over the door is a nuclear bunker. We had them underneath all the large buildings and factories at home. The government said it was to protect us from the Americans, who wanted to destroy everything east of NATO's borders."

"True, true," agreed Magda. "But it's the other way round now. Russia is the barbarian now."

170

"That's the way of the world, that's what I'm saying," mumbled Rula, her eyes closing.

"Good job I'm driving," remarked Magda, in an aside to me. "Did you make these cakes?"

"I most certainly did…and didn't you know that partaking of cannabinoids is a good inhibitor against road rage? Look at her, she's at peace, she'd be fine behind the wheel." Rula was a most exceptional looking woman, that was true, but only an unreconstructed male would think such a thing these days, or so they say.

I've been cooking up the stuff since I had a job in Glasgow, a summer job many years ago. City life depressed me and a spliff in the evening or some well-infused baking was my way of forgetting the crush of people on the noxious underground and the rumble of traffic. I use it only during holidays now; I had promised myself I'd limit my use once I found the gun in the drawer. You need a clear head if you carry a gun. Both the girls smoked it, I was aware, it helped them put their less pleasant daily experiences behind them. Secretly, while I thought their use of the stuff okay, I hoped they never progressed to anything stronger. That would be the end of their good looks. Anyway, Benny forbade them doing stronger drugs in his premises and I'm sure they kept to that because they respected him.

With daylight almost gone, they decided to leave, the roads were going to be tricky with the ice rehardening, and as they left, Rula brightened and hugged me. "Don't be anywhere else but here on Hogmanay," she instructed with a grin. "I'll have a special surprise for you to mark bringing in the new year." What was I to make of that—or her? My brain was too misted by delta-9 THC to ponder it any further.

So my Christmas evening was spent with one or two of my special homebakes and Sniffer's warm body curled up beside me, thinking about that situation room, which would have been located in the basement bunker if Rula's nuclear conjecture had been correct. But what kind of situation was it for, it didn't look heavily defended. With my light-headed thoughts, it took a while to realise that Sniffer was standing up at the lounge window barking, with his head under the curtain. A rap on the window came again, an insistent tap with a ring finger that would not be ignored, and I took some deep breaths upon standing before going to look. Outside, I was half surprised and half not to see what was a very cold-looking Major Frisk, dressed only in a tweed jacket and cavalry twills.

Peremptorily, he thrust a bottle at me and I noticed he had another in his other fist. "What's going on up there," he demanded, stamping his boots on my front door mat. "Up at the new house. There's blood on the east corridor floor and no sign of Evangeline."

"I take it you've been in, then."

"Of course I've bloody been in. What do you take me for, psychic?"

"Sorry. I didn't know you had a key."

He sighed with exasperation but I couldn't catch up with his mood, I was still adrift.

"No key. It's all codes up there, damn it. Didn't she give it to you, 696969?"

Soixante neuf three times over, I'd remember that, I'd enjoyed several of them.

"I'd been helping her move in," he explained. "Never forget a number. Top of the class at Arithmetic. But what has happened to the old gal? It didn't look good up there."

"You've not heard from Alan Mackie, then." As I spoke those words I wondered whether I was compromising Alan in any way; but fuck him, why should I care?

"That young man's too big for his boots. No, I've been expecting him to report in this past week." The major looked fit to burst a vein in his forehead, he was tight with ire and I wondered if I should offer him one of my cakes.

"Well," I said instead, "Mrs Delacroix is dead, I'm afraid. An accident. Self-inflicted wounds."

That seemed to deflate his anger even quicker than would have ingesting a cannabis cake. He stumbled into my lounge and almost sat on poor Sniffer, both of them selecting the same armchair.

"Dead? And I was bringing her some Christmas cheer." He held up the other bottle and I saw it had a saltire as its label colours, as did mine when I looked. "Good whisky," he explained. "She liked a drop, you know."

"I think it was brandy that led to her demise," I volunteered.

"Hmmm," he murmured. "Bloody French. And was the unquenchable Alan there at the time? Is that where he's been hiding, up at the new place? With his bum chums no doubt."

"He's abroad, I believe. Some sort of training."

He raised his eyebrows at that. "D'you know, ambitious Mr Mackie has awarded himself the rank of captain. Captain, I ask you! All on account of some tomfoolery with a pretend explosive device. Well, his chums like it but the Board hasn't approved it yet."

Frisk looked around the room searchingly. "Well, if you're not planning to open that bottle I think I'll be on my way. Best get home to bed after this unfortunate news. I hate bloody Christmas anyway, all that phony bonhomie and unwanted gifts. Evangeline chose the right time to make an exit if you ask me. Poor bloody woman, she had no family— I think we were her family, actually, the Saltire." He stood and shook hands. "I hope you'll come to think of us that way too, in time."

He stroked Sniffer's ears, went to the door and bade farewell. "I expect I'll hear all about it from the Captain," he sniffed. "Tootle-pip." Then he was nothing more than the sound of boots marching away over the crunching ice on my front drive.

So that was my Ghost of Christmas Present—or so it seemed when my head cleared about three in the morning. The criticism of Alan Mackie was the headline in my memory, I'd had the false impression he was the Saltire's blue-eyed boy. And it was possible I'd be seeing him today. I went to have a shave and just laughed and laughed with my doppelganger in the mirror.

13

As it happened, Alan Mackie didn't arrive at my door on Boxing Day. I had underestimated the distance he'd be travelling, and of course I had no flight details. I spent the day finishing the much-delayed clear-out of my parents' belongings, and hoped the next week would bring one of those doorstep charity collections.

When he did appear, late on the afternoon of the following day, he looked deeply tanned, but his otherwise hale and hearty appearance was subverted by the way he clutched his shoulder and winced as he sat down at my kitchen table.

"Shrapnel," he gave one word in explanation before I inquired.

"You've been in a war zone?"

"I've been in a foolish zone," he grimaced. "Never try to show off your juggling skills with a live grenade."

I put Major Frisk's whisky bottle on the table, and his eyes lit up when he saw the label. "This might help," I suggested, pouring him a double.

"Indeed it might," he quipped. "So you have joined us after all." But seeing my bemused expression he continued, indicating the bottle with a nod: "The Saltire. You are one of us now, yes?"

"No," I answered.

"Oh, only when…"

"It was a gift. From Major Frisk."

He frowned. "Frisk's been sniffing around has he? Did you tell him about Evangeline? He was fond of her, we all knew that, but he was very professional about it. After all, she was his boss, so to speak."

My silence was eloquent.

"She was the Saltire's Chairman, or we should say Chair in these gender sensitive days I suppose. Not the CEO, not active, but a bit of a fixer for us nevertheless, she knows a lot of people in high places. You weren't aware, obviously."

I wondered if my father had been aware. Remembering his dislike of anything remotely military, including private militia, I don't think he would have approved.

"So, what's been going on?" He was visibly eager to know. "I think you mentioned it was self-inflicted. Does that mean it was suicide? Only she's been rather flaky of late."

I told him the whole bizarre story of the errant pheasant and the Duchess's drunken reaction. I even mentioned the matter of the broken automatic weapon, and he shook his head in puzzlement.

"She kept saying she wanted to have one," he said. "She was convinced she was under surveillance and needed something more effective than a shotgun for protection."

He sat for a moment and I refilled his glass. Then his expression darkened.

"This business about selling the house, well, you can't."

He sounded as if he was uttering an imperative.

"And how is that?"

"I'm sure you've been and had a look around."

I nodded, cautiously.

"And?"

"Well, it had always struck me that it was too large a place for a woman on her own; and the security infrastructure, the stockade and everything, it all seemed unnecessary for a private home."

"Yes, but what did you think once you'd looked around?"

"My uncertainty was confirmed by the premises looking more like an office environment than a dwelling house."

"That's all? Look, stop behaving like a stuffy old fool. Don't you see why I'm saying you can't sell it?"

"The Situation Room, the server installation in the basement. Is that what you mean?"

"Ah, so you have had a good poke at the place. Impressed?"

"That's not the word I would have chosen, although I admit it did look rather smart."

"My command centre," Alan sat back proudly. Yes, Frisk was right about his arrogance.

"Yours?"

"Well, the North East Chapter's."

"I thought the Saltire was headquartered in Edinburgh."

"And so it is. I didn't say this was a headquarters, but a command centre. A central point from which to command operations. We have others in other regions of Scotland. It would be too open to scrutiny if it was located in one of the cities. The data centre in the basement, though, that's Saltire Central's. Best kept away from HQ's systems, less likely to be a target for hacking. We have set up some anonymous floating IP addresses for the client stations. Can't put everything in the cloud for obvious reasons."

177

I just had to ask and I knew he was waiting for my question. "Just what operations are you expecting to command?"

"Can we sit somewhere a little more comfortable?" he asked, rubbing his shoulder, "and I'll tell all."

We went through to the lounge and he sat back on a heap of cushions with a groan.

"I get the impression you don't follow the news much," he began, "you always sound fairly peripheral when it comes to politics."

I nodded, silently. He was correct there. I found it too depressing to keep up with current affairs in the newspapers or by watching the news on television, yet some snatches still got through from talking to my brother or Benny. Russians murdering and raping in eastern Europe, the absurdities of the Woke, the nasty party in government at Westminster, it was all too much darkness with which to burden myself unnecessarily.

"Okay," said Alan, "well you know our underlying objective, an independent Scotland." I nodded assent once more. "But by your own admission just now, I doubt you know what the true economic situation is across Great Britain—the name of which is actually one very pertinent inaccuracy, for it's no longer great, and Scotland's at risk of going down the pan with the rest of the union."

"You know that for sure do you?"

"Just listen. You'll be aware of rocketing prices at the moment, I imagine, but you probably won't have heard that Britain's current account deficit is 8.3% of GDP. I don't suppose that figure means much to you, it probably doesn't sound like much, but it's the worst since records began. The

178

UK government's apologists blame the domestic situation on soaring energy costs, the after effect of the pandemic, Russian imperialism, weak world markets and supply chain inefficiencies. But the real cause is Brexit, which that same government forced upon Scotland. Brexit is having a massively deleterious effect on UK exports and inward investment. We voted against Brexit, didn't we, they ignored us, and now we're being punished by it. We have to cut adrift. We need to regain access to our largest market, the European Union, and we're going to have to do that alone, as dogma in both parties at Westminster is set against it."

I didn't interrupt. He was in full flow. I felt I was back to my student days.

"On top of that, you know what the Russians are up to, trying to re-establish their old borders, well we don't only need price stability and growth from being with our European neighbours, we also need to be with them in the European political framework, in order to enjoy collective security."

"That all sounds like the datasheet for a manifesto, Alan." I didn't mean to sound scornful.

He laughed. "I suppose it did, but it's the reality we are preparing to escape, to fight our way out of the box. Our new CEO, Culzean, is poised to blow the whistle any day soon."

Alan sat back and watched me, quietly. I knew he was expecting a response, and I could tell he'd been wanting to thrust that little polemic at me for some time.

"Am I expected to have been drawn to the cause by all that? Were you recruiting just now?"

He smiled. "Well, you're the man with a gun. Someone who walks around with a handgun in his pocket is hardly likely to be a supporter of the establishment. A man of emotion, too, although you probably deny that characteristic, someone who'll not hesitate to confront any attempt to degrade your way of life. That's your trigger, there has always to be an element of emotion. We've spoken about that before."

He could see he'd touched a sensitive point, but went on, despite my silence.

"Doesn't what the nasty party have done to our country set your temper hurtling skyward? I know it does by the set of your mouth. Look, we need people like you. And in addition, you're now the sole custodian of our arms cache. I'd feel much more comfortable that you were looking after us as a fellow of the movement instead of an outsider who's doing it simply from obligation."

I needed to side-step his pressure. I wanted to think about it on my own, or discuss it with Rula. Oh hang, why on earth would I want to discuss it with her?

"The weapons, you're not planning to transfer them to your command centre?"

"Hell no, they're safer where they are. The new house will be too busy, they'd be less secure with all sorts coming and going. Besides, there's no appropriate space." He shrugged, wincing at the movement. "No, they're to stay in your assured custody. But, having mentioned your having a gun I would, all the same, like to offer you some training, teach you to use something a bit more potent. It will give you a greater sense of certitude in the face of danger, for I can promise you, danger is coming."

"Okay," I conceded at last, "give me until New Year to consider everything you said. I don't like to be rushed."

He seemed pleased that he'd made some progress but I wasn't yet a convert. Nonetheless, I agreed to accompany him on some shooting practice. It wouldn't be a wasted skill, especially if he was right about what was coming. We arranged to meet at Knock Hall in a day's time.

We spent a whole two days before Hogmanay, most of the time flat on our stomachs, in the cold wet grass of the meadow below the new house. As arranged, Alan had met me in front of Knock Hall; he'd lain two guns on the bench beside the door, two Heckler & Koch HK33s I later learned. I made a mental note to ask for the key that he'd used to gain entry to the Hall.

First showing me how to carry one safely, we each took a weapon and crossed over the slippery Avenue into the meadow. Deer moved like shadows in the early morning frosted mist and we shouted and waved to move them on, not wanting to create any unintended victims of our sport. For that's how I approached it, with Alan my coach rather than my commander, for wasn't shooting a legitimate sport, although not usually with guns of this calibre?

He'd set up some targets at the bottom end of the field, images of the prime minister's head mounted on straw bales, with a dense grassy bank behind that shielded us from the farm road, as it swung around to the crossroads. "Now," said Alan, "when you show me you can consistently hit him between the eyes I'll know that you've done enough—for today. But we need to move back there first, from here it's too much like kids' play."

We retreated through the grass and Alan bade me note the distance he had brought us back from the target. "This is as close as you would ever want to be in an exchange of fire," he said. "Any closer and your enemy has the opportunity to distract you—by sudden feints or vocally, for instance. Like this we can remain detached; if you can't hear their voice or see the fear in their eyes you'll never come to think of the target as a fellow human being." It made sense to me, though if I was fired up to kill, like when the dognapper grabbed Sniffer, there was nothing in the way of deliberate distraction that would stop me, I was sure of that. "But," he added, "if you find yourself so close you can hear the fellow breathe, it's better to have a supplementary." He rolled up his trouser leg to reveal a knife in a leather sheath, strapped to his ankle, and nodded to me knowingly. You're a real snake, mister, I decided. But a smart cookie all the same.

It was an enjoyable two days, I have to admit, despite the cold, but we were blessed with two of those glorious east coast winter days when the sun is out and the air is dry, and the crack of our gunfire melded with the intermittent gunshots of men away in the fields by the river, hunting rabbit and pheasant in the easy lull of the interlude between Christmas and New Year. We were fortunate that the Avenue was glazed hard with ice, for it deterred walkers, and on the other flank we were shielded from the farm road by a compact barrier of hornbeam and beech.

"You done good," said Alan at the end of the two days. "I'd be happy for you to watch my back in a conflict situation." I wasn't sure myself that I was yet that good, but I had made progress with a new weapon and reckoned I could acquit myself if threatened.

"So, have you made up your mind?" he asked. "About joining us."

I reminded him about my need to think it over and that there was Hogmanay to see through first.

"And what are your plans?" he asked, "for seeing in the new year? Anything arranged, or are you planning to spend the evening in front of the television watching Hootenanny and reviews of the year?" He groaned. "Personally I loathe all that looking back over the twelvemonth, all that maudlin reminiscence about celebrities who've died, tragedies in Africa, you know the sort of thing."

It was how I felt too, but I had another arrangement, which I told him, omitting of course Rula's promise.

"She's a fine woman," he remarked, replicating my own thoughts, "not that I'd be interested, but she looks good. Pity she's a tart."

"You know that do you?"

He just shook his head as if in disbelief at my presumed innocence.

"Every man—or in this case, woman—to his own," I rebutted him. "Why would it matter when, as you say, she's a fine woman?"

14

Rula did indeed look gorgeous when she stepped out from her Porsche onto my drive on that last evening of the year, although her first words kind of spoiled the illusion of a princess.

"Fucking roads haven't been gritted," she yelled. "Look at that wheel!" But she soon forgot the damage caused when she'd hit a bollard on the main road, she didn't really hold a lot of store for material objects, which was one thing that drew me to her. The clinch that she held me in, there in the freezing air—it was minus ten!—was both passionate and curiously spousal. It was also surprisingly exhilarating, there were notes in that feeling that were new to me. All that gunfire must have shaken up my brain.

Wrapped in her white sheepskin coat and hood, beneath which a gaily decorated peasant's smock blazed with flowers, she made me think of Mucha's painting of Winter. But she was her own scene of natural beauty, not a copy. There was nothing there to whisper the name of her trade, in fact she could have come straight from Hollywood. Truth to tell, the dolls who preen and smirk in their expensive gowns on the red carpet at the Oscars often look far more like a common hooker than did Rula.

I made us a shakshuka for our meal, only it turned out to be more a frittata, but she didn't care. Then we sat and drank port and shared a humungous spliff. Rula curled up next to me on the sofa, much to Sniffer's chagrin, her long legs coiled around mine, and we talked of everything and nothing as friends will do. As time passed and we took a break from a long spell of kissing I asked if she wanted to go upstairs, but she said no and, mysteriously, it was to be strictly eleven-thirty before we retired to the bedroom.

She gave an enigmatic smile and, *apropos* of nothing, commenced telling me a curious tale about her childhood, a time when she kept chickens and goats and used to be beaten for refusing to kill them in hard times when the family needed to eat. I tried to work out how that had produced the Rula I had come to know but only managed to attach the image she'd drawn to her persistent good nature. I was also wondering what was the special surprise she'd brought me. Had she forgotten to bring it from her car?

I was showing signs of being sleepy (I'm an early morning rather than late night soul) when she took my hand and we climbed the stairs. The special surprise presumably could wait until morning.

"Please leave the television on," she said, "just in the background."

"But it's that bloody Hootenanny garbage," I protested, slipping into bed.

"Leave it on," she said, sternly.

We just lay there for some time in a warm mellow cocoon of soft skin and duvet. She turned to whisper in my ear:

"Hey, darling, just so you know, I've been off the pill for the past month." Her words were soft and benign—and curious. "I've had no clients for the same time too, longer in fact."

The impact of her admission was immediate and I started up.

"So, we'd better refrain from—"

"Hush," she smiled and pulled me down upon her.

The wittering of the MC on the television and the blare of brassy jazz did not impede our lovemaking. And strangely, the fact that there could be consequences gave our coupling an unusual frisson of excitement, our pulses quickening in tandem with the heat of our vigour, whilst far away on the television the MC was talking and I could hear a rise in chatter from the audience.

"How are you doing?" Rula whispered demandingly.

"Pretty good," I gasped. Actually, the moment was becoming critical.

"Same with me," she said, breathing heavily and glancing at the clock by the bed. From the television, we heard begin a raucous countdown to the new year. "Be with me, will you?" she pleaded. Her movements and her words were now most urgent.

In no time at all, Rula tensed and arched her back at the moment the bongs from Big Ben rang out and I joined her in our mutual cries of joy.

"Happy new year," she laughed, kissing me, her tongue hot and vigorous, those long legs made fast around me, her fingers on the back of my neck. "We made it through together. Are we not good together?"

I could not argue with that, but whether her special surprise had been our mutual orgasm or her declaration of unconstrained fecundity, right then I could not, would not attempt to decide. I just felt happy, extraordinarily happy, to be here at this time with this woman, physically and emotionally joined in the moment. It was not the time for cold reflection but deep in my head I could hear the sound of someone shredding my convictions regarding love and lust, and the snap of a manacle closing.

Rula had determined, it turned out, that this would be her own time of renewal and new beginnings. It was one New Year resolution that was not going to lapse, I could tell.

"I'm no longer a working girl," she asserted. "That was last year. This year I shall be…well, let's wait and see. But I'm nobody's creature, not anymore."

I promised to tell Benny for her, I hadn't yet mentioned the girls' restlessness. Rula was afraid he'd be angry to have lost one of his prime assets. And whilst I was in an accommodating mood she persuaded me to let her stay for a while, until she found her own place she said, she couldn't stay on at her apartment over the burger shop, it wouldn't be right with Magda continuing to trade. Although, as she confided to me later, Magda was also on the verge of quitting, which I already suspected from their conversation just prior to Christmas.

So, life went on through January and February in a kind of easy routine. Walks with Sniffer in the wide open spaces locally; visits to the village coffee shop for a lazy brunch, where Rula's elegantly slim and glossy presence as my regular companion raised some eyebrows, for she had striking looks and an enviable poise, whereas I was just a malcontent approaching middle age with long hair and a reputation as something of a loner. But all seemed fine throughout that time despite me suffering my perennial sense of apprehension.

Something bad would happen, things couldn't go on being this good. My inner voice had always reminded me that doom always lurked somewhere up ahead. But nothing terrible happened. Just I noticed that Sniffer was slowing up, at ten he was irrevocably tagged a senior, and he'd come back from his walks with his tongue on the ground and dragging his hind legs. I committed to reduce the length and exuberance of his walks (some chance!) and sent off for a tub of joint supplement. Rula too was ailing for a couple of weeks, throwing up noisily in the mornings, but it didn't last and the bug she must have caught on one of our outings seemed not to be interested in me.

We'd settled into something of a routine and I woke one morning after an unsettling dream, worrying about that very fact. Had I found myself new shackles? Delightful though Rula was, she hadn't done much about finding somewhere to live and I began to feel oppressed by her constant presence, whilst feeling bad about thinking such a thing.

Rula instinctively knew what was going through my mind, for over breakfast she raised the subject of our relationship and reiterated the declaration of love she had made those months ago.

"I love you," she confirmed, "of that do not doubt me, but I make no claim on you. Go where you will in the world I shall always love you, but I'll never use the ties of love to reel you back in."

I heard her words and silently squeezed her hand. It was enough of an acceptance for her and she smiled quietly.

My other ongoing source of disquiet was Alan Mackie and the Saltire. I'd enjoyed the time I'd spent in the meadow learning to use a powerful weapon, but the thought of actually joining the Saltire as a member just didn't fit with my predilections. Since a child I'd never enjoyed being part of a team, the adherent of a club or a society. It had marked me out as an outsider at school and university, but I'd always rather liked the inverse celebrity it gave me.

On New Year's day, Alan had telephoned to tell me he was off to South America on business, but would see me on his return in around ten weeks. So what had happened to the insurrection, rebellion, or whatever it was his CEO had been anxious to kick off?

"A man in his position will choose the right moment in his own time," he assured me, "but what about you? Have you reached a decision? It's New Year."

I gave him a decisive no, at which he wanted to know if I'd moved into Knock Hall yet. Again, I answered that I had not, since I was waiting to hear from the Duchess's notary to confirm the inheritance. That brought a torrent of expletives and the threat that I'd better be ensconced there when he returned, or he'd—I won't repeat what terrors he predicted heaping upon me, but I'm pleased to say I still have my genitals, eyes and ears. As it happened, he didn't turn up at my house until we'd ticked off twelve weeks of the year on the wall calendar. Time was flashing by and, immediately before Alan returned from whatever mischief saw him in Europe, some rather extraordinary things befell Rula and me.

15

Around the time we were expecting Alan Mackie to roll up like a bad penny at our door we had an unexpected visitor. Sniffer did his loud announcement that there was someone at the front door, he'd heard a rattling at the letterbox and he was going to tear them to shreds. So Rula quit looking at the property ads online and went to see what all the fuss was about. I heard her unlock the door and then give a sharp shriek, before running back down the hall to the kitchen, where I was writing.

"It's Big Mac!" she hissed, visibly shaking.

"What? Where?"

"Out there, at the door." She pointed with one hand, the other clawing at her head with distraction.

But he wasn't out there. He'd followed Sniffer's welcoming tail down the hall and was shuffling his considerable bulk into my kitchen, where he stood awkwardly grinning.

"Ever so sorry," he rumbled, "but I seem to have upset the young lady. Thought I'd better see what was the matter."

"It's no matter," I answered, "she's just of a nervous disposition." I was hoping I could scoot him out of the house before matters between us deteriorated.

190

"Are you sure you're alright, hun," he asked Rula. "After all, I know I'm a big fella but I didn't think I looked that frightening." He peered searchingly at her then the lines on his face cleared as recognition spread through his eyes. "O lovey," he said, "you're just the girl I've been looking for these past weeks." He sat down with a thump on a kitchen stool, as if whatever fuelled his huge movements had been expended. "I've been hunting high and low for you," he explained. "I went over to Benny's but the guy I saw there said you'd gone away, he wasn't sure where. I have so wanted to say how sorry I am; for nicking your money and for what my brother did to you, of course. I've never hurt a defenceless woman, never would, and I'm ashamed on his behalf. Oh, I'm so glad to have found you at last."

Rula and I listened dumbstruck. It was the total reverse of a scene we'd rehearsed in our minds since we disposed of Ronnie, his brother.

I think Rula recovered her wits before I did, offering him a cup of tea, which he gratefully accepted. This was all so bizarre.

"I could do with a cuppa," he agreed. "It's still chilly out there and it feels like I've been stomping this village all day." He put his hands in the pocket of his overcoat and produced a bundle of leaflets. "I think there's one through every letterbox now," he said. "Except yours, of course. Here—" He passed us one each. They were 'Missing' notices, and bore a picture of his brother, Ronnie McAllister. A reward of £500 was offered for information leading to the successful discovery of Ronnie's current known whereabouts.

"My brother," he explained. "All I know is that his stepson accompanied him to that big house up there but came

191

away on his own. There was some kind of altercation with a particular young bastard—excuse my French—a scoundrel with whom I happen to be familiar, who threatened our lad with a gun. If I see him again, I've more than one reason to send him six foot under, I can tell you. But the one I do want to see is my brother, for all that he's a violent misogynist—sorry again, Miss. That's why I'm posting these flyers everywhere in the vicinity. The police aren't interested in doing anything—and why would they be when Ronnie is someone they'd be keen to see the back of?"

He paused to sip his tea and Rula and I glanced at each other with expressions of relief.

Big Mac was evidently feeling relaxed in our warm kitchen and made no move to leave. He put his cup down and prepared to talk further, starting with a belch and a big breath.

"Beg pardon," he gasped. "I drink too fast, but I'm always on the go, rarely have time to sit like this. As I was saying, I'm looking for my brother, Ronnie—they call me Big Mac, by the way, on account of me being—well, big. I wasn't able to join the search any sooner, only I was locked up on remand all that time. Jesus, you wouldn't believe how slowly the wheels of justice turn. Anyway, you may have read about the case, a misunderstanding about dodgy money and then I was accused of supplying drugs through my dance clubs—I've got two in Aberdeen."

He talked on unbroken, we were able only to interject murmurs of surprise or agreement.

"However," he took up again after a quick gulp of tea, "I was eventually acquitted of the drug offence. Turned out it was my site manager who was the culprit, he was a member of some shitty political group and was storing drugs for them in the cellar of one of the clubs." He sighed. "My favourite, the Purple Rooster. Y'know, I saw that little scrote there, the supplier, on a number of occasions, same scoundrel who threatened our kid by the description, he was there quite brazenly conniving with my manager. Cocky git, he introduced himself to me as Captain something or other. I hope he gets court marshalled when they learn what he's been up to. You don't expect that sort of thing from the military, do you?"

"I think you said it was a political group, not army."

"I did, didn't I? Well it was, one of those special units I suppose. Whatever, I won't forget that face in a hurry, horrible great scar down one side of his face. I can't have been the first person whose business he'd shat on."

"So you were judged not guilty in the end." I was trying to get him to wrap up. This was all getting too close to home.

"Aye, but my manager, the idiot, he was sent down. All that happened to me was time wasted in the nick and losing my club licence. I dunno what happened about the dodgy banknotes, there'd been some trouble at the bank in Union Street, I think there's a much bigger investigation going on. These things can take years. But my solicitor is handling it."

"It's lucky they didn't keep you for years," offered Rula. "Being locked away from the rest of the world is no fun, I know."

"Aye, you're right. But I did have some moments of light and edification."

Rula's look of interest encouraged him and I scowled at her.

"There was this priest," he began, and my heart sank. "Do you know, I always thought of priests as composed sort of

193

blokes, serene even. But this one, he was a mess. It was his job to come round and talk to us, make sure we weren't suffering, going mental and such from the incarceration and everything. We didn't have to be Catholics, he'd give succour, as he called it, to anyone. But this poor geezer, he was suffering himself. He'd been banging some nun at the convent, he admitted, and couldn't live with the guilt. He reckoned he was a sex addict, although I don't think there's such a thing, we all like to fuck, don't we? Well, I didn't know what to say, yet he came to see me more and more frequently, he was looking for help himself. So, I told him, if being a priest and a sex addict don't work, you have to resolve to stop being one or the other. It only takes will power and stamina, and having had a religious life must have proved he possessed both of those. Well, maybe he had, but he was poor at the old decision making."

"Anyway, to cut a long story short, and I'm sure you want to have your place to yourself again." He stood, thought, and sat down again. "My friendly priest came in one morning all cock-a-hoop and lively, saying he'd been chatting to some professor type who said he didn't have to renounce God in order to enjoy sex, he could simply transfer to a different and more tolerant religion. So, how about this, he was off to become a Buddhist. Apparently they're all at it like rabbits, Buddhists, or so he told me."

I shouldn't have accused Benny of making up a tall story. I wondered if the bit about the novitiate was true; but I couldn't ask Magda to corroborate that. Yet it was still an amusing tale, and I was beginning to enjoy Big Mac's company now that I knew he wasn't all thug.

By now, it was late afternoon and we took some drinks and cake out into the conservatory—not cannabis cake on this occasion but a rich simnel that Rula had made. She was clearly enjoying having some company in the house and wanted to talk further. It was then that Mac confided that as a consequence of his conversations with the priest he had himself joined the International Society for Consciousness, a group I had known about as the Hare Krishna movement. I'd seen them on the streets of a city in England, all flowing orange robes, sandals and finger cymbals. Soft in the head but harmless, had been my assessment.

"It's done wonders for my state of mind," he admitted. "I'm a changed man, I've got empathy at last. I used to be a pretty unpleasant character, come to think of it; a sociopath someone called me, or was it psychopath? One of them I'm sure. Before I discovered the movement, I'd never have been able to sit down here with two strangers and have a good natter. But you're no strangers to me, we are all brothers and sisters on this planet. We have to stick together, support each other against the evil in the world."

It was a philosophy I knew I could never take on and I saw Rula grinning cheekily at me.

"That's another reason I've been looking around these parts," he said, "but the right property is scarce and the prices are just stupid." He saw I didn't follow. "You see, things generally have been looking up in this area and we're wanting a quiet site on which to build a meditation centre. At the moment, converts have to go all the way to Perth, and we have decided to provide facilities more locally. There are also a lot of busy business folk, non-members that is, all kinds looking for a long weekend of solitary meditation, under guidance from practitioners in meditation and mindfulness like us." He coloured. "Well, I'm no expert yet, but I'm getting there."

I suppose that was the moment when months of mental turmoil came to a stop and I took breath. I remembered Magda's 'simple solution', her suggestion for how I could start my life anew, how to free myself from the responsibilities that I had never sought. More than that, how also to launch Rula on the journey of independence that she'd been seeking, it was all here, laid out unwittingly by this man we had initially thought of as a threat. I could almost hear the pieces locking into place in the hothouse of my imagination.

"So, you have moved on from the dance club business?"

"As I said, they won't renew my licence when it comes up next month. I don't have the time anyway, now I'm with the brothers and sisters."

"But it must have been a profitable business, what with all the students we have in Aberdeen." I hoped I wasn't sounding obvious.

"Aye, it was that, but my mission is now to build up an income stream for the Society. Hence the meditation centre."

I went and let Sniffer into the garden for a toilet break. This promising thought process couldn't be rushed.

"So who have you got managing the Purple Rooster these days, surely it needs constant attention?"

"My Missus, but she hates it, all the young bloods strutting and preening. Can't wait till we get shot of the place—both places actually."

I took a slow breath and tried hard to sound nonchalant.

"Any buyers lined up?"

"Pah, time wasters, that's all. Everyone wants something for nothing these days."

"Well," I said calmly, "I might be able to help you there. I have a property that could well suit your needs. It's nearby, a large, brand new modern house with office space, located in a secluded rural spot a short walk from here. There's even some serious IT infrastructure." Rula's eyes were popping open like organ stops. "Could be just the place for a meditation centre. If you like it, I'll do a swap for your two clubs."

Big Mac's face looked ready to split from the astonished smile upon his mouth.

"I'm pretty certain you wouldn't lose financially on such a deal," I said encouragingly but probably unnecessarily. "The site has open land in front of it and is surrounded by mature trees. For reasons I won't explain now, it has security fencing that may make you feel more private, and there is but one house nearby and a farm."

I couldn't have done better if I'd actually set out to stop him in his tracks with a bullet.

Rula filled Mac's glass and he sat open-mouthed for several minutes. Then he started nodding, rocking in the wicker chair that he'd surely fitted only with great perseverance, then he began to laugh, his legs out straight in front of him. "Oh, how Krishna smiles on me today," he bellowed, "thank you lord, thank you. And thank you too," he said to me, "most certainly I will look kindly on this unexpected offer. It will be a great weight off my shoulders to say farewell to my two businesses. The end of a not entirely fortunate era. When may I see this magical place?"

We agreed on the following day for his introduction to the ugly house, as I'd come to refer to it with Rula. With an enthusiastic shaking of hands and a decorous kiss for Rula, he took his leave, a happier man than he'd expected to be when he set out on the day's gloomy leafleting trail.

"Well, he seemed a nice sort," commented Rula when the man had gone.

"'Seemed' is the word," I answered her. "I don't mean to be churlish, but you can never be completely sure of a submissive dog, not even Sniffer. And remember, just a few hours ago you were scared out of your wits by the sight of him."

She shook her head. "Do you always think the worst of everyone?"

"In your case, no, but you've not given me cause—yet."

She stamped her feet and made a fist, with a shout of mock frustration that made Sniffer bark. Then, "If that's what you think of the big loon, are you certain about doing a deal with him?"

"It solves several predicaments: his, mine and yours. It's too much of any easy solution for him and, when he sees the place he'll know who has the better end of the bargain, at least in cash terms, and cash is what he's looking to generate."

"But my predicament—how come?" She was looking disputatious.

"How'd you like to have your own dance club? There's one for Magda too. You both keep saying you need a new challenge."

For the sake of avoiding becoming the tiresome narrator of interpersonal frivolities, I won't describe in detail the course of her consequent cry of 'Wowsers', to the hug that grew into a kiss, that became a...no, as I intimated—one has to preserve a morsel of privacy.

198

Big Mac took the bus back to Aberdeen that evening but his return was chauffeured the next day by his nephew, the first we knew of it being the throb of an over-tuned engine in my drive, where from the bedroom window I saw Mac alight from the garish yellow car with the big exhaust. Fortunately, we were spared a meeting with Ronnie's stepson, the car reversing at speed and intimidating a neighbour's cat as it sped away. Mac saw me at the window and waved a bunch of papers at me.

"Tell me I wasn't dreaming yesterday evening," he insisted, bustling through to the kitchen. "On the chance I wasn't, I've brought some documents you'll need, including last year's figures. All legit. My accountant's letter is in there somewhere." He pointed over his shoulder with his thumb, in the direction of the yellow car's exhaust roar, "That's our Ronnie's boy. He'll come back for me later. I don't drive, see."

It wasn't stated but I had no doubts that Big Mac had taken my offer firmly on board, and only disappointment with the ugly house itself was going to change his mind. I decided we'd walk to it, so he would be able to appreciate the seclusion of the site within the context of the village, and he agreed that would be a wise thing to do. Thus it was, for as we left the last village house behind and ambled north along Knockhall Road, past the blossom on the wild plum and hawthorn trees, with sheep munching the new grass in the fields, the morning felt calm and there came a soft light through the leaves to encourage us along our way.

"I see you're carrying," he said, right out of the blue, and pointed at my sagging jacket pocket. "Unless it's a very big key to open the front door."

"No key," I answered. "Keyless entry. And yes, you've found me out." Patting my pocket I hoped I'd closed the subject.

"So what are you not telling me?" he persisted. "This doesn't look to be a rough area."

"It isn't. I'm not hiding anything from you. It's just me and my quarrel with the world."

"Hah." Mac scratched his chin. "That used to be me. You should become a Buddhist. Sort out any quarrels."

Just then the top of the ugly house appeared over the distant hedge of the barley field we were passing, the offending asymmetric window shining brightly in the morning sun.

"Is that it?" he asked. "Amazing, from upstairs you'd be able to see all the way down here and across to…what's over there?" He pointed over to our right.

"That's the nature reserve and the estuary."

"Nature, great, no settlements nearby, just peace and privacy. And you can see all around I betcha."

"Look." I pointed out the ruined castle on the rise behind the ugly house. "That's why they built that there. It has an uninterrupted view all the way to the sea. That'll be your view too."

He quickened his step and in minutes I was pressing three times soixante-neuf on the keypad at the front door.

"Cheeky," he laughed. His upbeat mood lasted throughout our tour of the house and was there still when later we sat in the kitchen at home.

I don't believe in the mystical power of coincidences, there's nothing uncanny about them, they're just the way things fall sometimes in a chaotic world, but on occasion their appearance can be very welcome. Finding a letter from the notary had been delivered whilst we were out, confirming my right of inheritance, was almost good enough to make me believe that coincidences have their toes in the tide of fate. Whatever may be on that score, it was enough for me to proceed with the exchange I'd proposed to Big Mac and we shook on the deal right there and then. Our solicitors could deal with the legal hoops and hurdles in their own time, transferring the rights to the house over to the Hare Krishna movement and the two dance clubs each to Rula and Magda. It just needed Mac and me to put our signatures on the requisite dotted lines somewhere.

I'd hardly had time to take my coat off when two things happened then that I'm sure had little to do with coincidence and everything to do with fate. The first was the roar of a motor vehicle arriving in my drive, where I could see its orange glow refracted in the frosted pane of the kitchen door.

"He won't come in," said Mac. "He's not one for company since his stepdad disappeared. A sad state of affairs. No, he'll just sit and wait for me."

The second was someone abusing the knocker on my front door and Sniffer's crazy howl of alert. I opened it to find Alan Mackie storming into my hall, almost spitting the words, "What's that fucking car doing out there?" It wasn't the pleasantest of reunions.

I put my finger to my lips and indicated the open door to the kitchen. He seemed to grasp my meaning, straightened his jacket and stepped quietly after me. Things didn't stay quiet for long.

"Hello, Captain," said Big Mac, standing. In order to make the most of his size, I guessed.

201

"Oh, long time no see," answered Alan, blanching, and glaring at Rula and me with a huge question mark in his eyes. I scowled at his tiresome cliché and he looked even more puzzled.

"That's because I've been inside for several months," replied Mac cuttingly. "Thanks to you, you despicable little fucker."

Alan reeled back against the kitchen table, as if he'd been shot. "But…"

"No," yelled Mac, "this is a butt, and I've been saving it for you." His headbutt was extraordinarily precise and heavy, I've always wondered how folk do it without hurting themselves, but I suppose Mac was adept after long years of practice. The blow for a moment looked as though it had made Alan's legs buckle but instead he lurched across the room with surprise and obvious pain. As he hit the glass in the door his hand went to the inside of his jacket and he recoiled from the door with his gun in his hand.

Now, I know I said that two things happened. Well, actually there were three, no four. Four things of significance, that is.

As he raised his gun and pointed it at Mac, Rula screamed—like a banshee, I thought afterwards—and, screaming, she kicked the gun out of his hand. I've always known she was athletic, but this was a real clincher, for as the gun spun in the air she dived and caught it, brought it close to her chest and—seemed totally at a loss what next to do with it.

She had little time to make a decision, for the kitchen door to the drive burst open and Mac's nephew, having no doubt heard the ruckus, burst in, throwing Alan across the room so that he collided with Mac, who pinned him against the wall. This energetic piece of choreography concluded when the boy recognised Rula, who was holding the gun, and he cried to Mac, "This is the bitch I told you about. She was there." He drew a wicked looking knife and clamped his arm around her neck, the knife held to her throat, her head thrown back and the gun falling from her hand. For the first time, I noticed that she was visibly in the family way.

It was quite a tense tableau, I can tell you. It was quickly even more strained when the boy saw Alan and hollered, "That's the cunt, that's him who threatened me, an' I reckon it was him killed my stepdad."

Big Mac was evidently struggling with his newly-adopted principles of peace and love. He'd punished Alan with that blow to the head, that had seemed sufficient, but what should he do now? He had the villain pinned to the wall, his hands around his throat (a family technique, I remarked to myself, obviously), but how to end it? Effectively, it was like he was holding a venomous snake, for Alan was not finished yet, and I recalled seeing that knife strapped to his leg. Big Mac was as stumped as had been Rula just moments before.

"Rip his fucking head off," urged the boy, a great example of today's articulate youth.

As for myself, I found myself fascinated by the dynamic geometry of the situation. Rula held at knifepoint, and Mac restraining Alan, whose old shoulder wound seemed to be bothering him, along with a newly bruised forehead. And then there was me, suspended in a passive corner to the three-way forcefield, standing with Sniffer at my feet by the kitchen peninsula. We made a very taut triangle, that was for certain. Very Tarantinesque, I noted with a smile.

It's funny what captures one's eye in such a situation, but there on the kitchen table, having somehow survived all the violent to-ing and fro-ing, was my letter from the notary and Mac's documents. There's such a lot that one can learn from the printed word; that idea came to me later in a kind of post-traumatic revelation.

Anyway, to continue…

Alan was choking, Mac's big hands had stayed where he put them, although when the big man saw me looking he relaxed his grip a little.

"Do something," wheezed Alan to me, "you're the man—"

I put my hand into my coat pocket and retrieved my gun. Everybody tensed and I shot Alan between the eyes. He had taught me well. The main thing is not to get distracted in a close situation.

It had indeed been a complex situation and sometimes complex situations are resolved by a single simple action. I had assessed the composition of the situation and decided which was the key pivot point. Killing Alan resolved the largest number of issues. It preserved my deal with Big Mac, which we yet had legally to conclude, it sustained Rula and Magda's new opportunity as club owners, and it ended my worries about being pressured to join the Saltire's enterprises. I would now sell the whole Knock Hall estate and be done with it all.

There remained, of course, the problem of Ronnie's stepson, who had recognised all three of us.

I begged to be excused for a moment and went upstairs, ostensibly to use the toilet. I came down with an old conference satchel stuffed with twenty pound notes and went up to the boy, who had released Rula but still held the knife.

"By the sound of it just now," I said to him, "I think your exhaust may be blown. Isn't it time to think about getting something a bit more classy. You don't want to be a kid forever, do you? You've got to take your dad's place in the world now. Here, this would buy you a Porsche or two, they're a great babe magnet if you're looking to impress classy women." I thrust the satchel at him and his jaw dropped. Money can buy almost anything or anyone, although appealing to the young man's sex drive was most likely what clinched his acquiescence. It's an irresistible motivator at that age.

16

We sat Alan's corpse in the passenger seat of Rula's Porsche and I followed in my old jalopy with Sniffer. He may be slowing up but he never likes to miss a chance to go over in the meadow after pheasants. We'd left Big Mac and the boy with an outsize pot of tea and a tin of cannabis cakes to recover themselves from all the excitement. With a colourful bandanna concealing the bullet hole in his forehead, the hubristic Captain took his last ride in style. There was surely room in a coffer at the end of that collapsing tunnel where we could leave him to the silverfish and spiders.

In fact, as we discovered, the far end of the tunnel had been even more seriously closed off by the sinkhole event that Alan had mentioned, but a large number of the Saltire munitions coffers remained accessible. We selected the container right at the end where he would just have to share the space with some of the Saltire's weapons, once we'd pulled out the top layer of guns. Now is that poetic justice or not? The rock ceiling creaked when we slammed down the lid, all very unstable, and we scarpered back up the slope in quick time. I'd be back the following day with an HK33 to bring down more of the roof.

My last four million I've spread between my brother, Rula and Magda, several animal charities and a nice packet to Benny. I've plenty in the bank myself now to keep me going, thanks to Benny. Knock Hall is on the market and Big Mac is scrutinising the bidders in order to make sure whoever buys it does not disrupt his peace and quiet in the ugly house. And, would you believe how neat this is, my father's old house where I'd been living is being rented by Ronnie's stepson, he likes being out in the country where he can hurtle his new Cayman GT4 around the quiet roads.

But what about all those guns in the tunnel under the Hall, I hear you ask, surely there would be a considerable cache remaining and recoverable in spite of the sinkhole collapse. Well, that is true, but any new owners can hardly ask Mrs Delacroix, the previous occupant, to explain them; they're not going to dig her up and demand 'madam, what were you doing with a subterranean armoury beneath your house?' Well, would they? No, seriously, I've contacted Major Frisk at Saltire HQ and passed him the dilemma. No-one could associate those guns with me. I've never lived there.

Frisk muttered that this was something for that no-good Mackie to deal with but, he complained, he's gone off somewhere again. Frisk has a while yet to move the guns out, all the same, the housing market is very slow just now. Or perhaps the Saltire itself will put in a bid for the estate, that would be a further neat solution. They don't seem to be getting very far with their revolution, as far as I can see, they might just want to keep their weapons a scary secret for a while longer.

So, I'm off to Ithaca, Greece, to join my friends who run a dog rescue charity across the Ionians. Well, I say friends, but it's really the dogs who are my mates rather than the people. You can never trust people. You can never entirely trust dogs either, as I may have remarked, but I'd rather face a growling dog with a juicy bone in my hand than some miscreant wielding a gun. I'd thought my long-held dream of moving to Greece had been dashed when the jingo-minded xenophobes severed our ties with Europe and the gift of freedom of movement was trashed; but I discovered that a shed-load of cash in the bank works wonders as a key to opening the door to foreign residency. So, yah boo to the bigots.

Rula urged me to go further than Greece. Be adventurous, she said, go east, see what Asia holds for you, there's nothing to keep you close to home. But I prefer to stay within the relatively civilised orbit of Europe. From India onwards lies barbarism. In the east, they have assumed the veneer of western culture, the shiny cars, advanced technologies and McDonalds fast food, but from Indonesia to Shanghai they still have pitiless dog meat farms and run those primitive wet markets. China even holds a cruel dog meat festival every year where these wonderful creatures are bludgeoned to death, to be barbecued as street food. They haven't learned, have they, that a dog is the greatest friend a man can have.

My brother was recently showing off to me about his new car. A flashy Korean copy of a Volkswagen Golf. I asked him if he felt comfortable to be driving a vehicle built by people who eat dogs. Considering the money I've given him he could have afforded something less ethically offensive. That really bugged me, seeing that car, although he was stroking Sniffer's silky ears at the time and did look a little uncomfortable when I spoke my mind. But, you see, it wasn't something he'd have thought about when the snake-tongued car salesman was explaining all the wonderful tech with which the car was loaded. I blame our schools myself for such ignorance; they just don't teach critical thinking. It's a pedagogical dereliction.

So, is that it then, the man with a gun, is that who you think I am? Huh, it's not that easy, is it? Anyway, I've left my gun, my father's gun, back in the sewing machine drawer. My brother can keep it as an heirloom when he finds it. His wife has long coveted the Singer and has found a craftsman in the village who's agreed to restore it, as a coffee table of all things. None so queer as folks, eh?

There's a cottage overlooking the harbour in Kioni village that I have my eye on. I hope Sniffer will get on with the cats that frequent the harbour bistros. But, I expect, now he's slowing up, that he'll spend a lot of his days just snoozing in the shade of an olive tree. My best friend, I say to him, it's advisable you don't hunt Greek pheasants, for sadly they're in decline; but you can paddle in the warm shallow waters of the beach to your heart's content.

Oh, and Rula has promised to visit me, once I'm settled in. She says it will be great to let the baby enjoy some sunshine after spending its first months in the cool of northeast Scotland. Oh well, I'm sure I can deal with that when the time comes. I'm not very child orientated, as you may have guessed, but to every problem there is a solution, isn't that the case? You just have to know what it is you want from life and when you want it.

I had a phone call this morning from my sister-in-law. She was sounding a little fraught. Apparently the police have been around to interview my brother. It seems some local artisan

209

found an unlicensed weapon and several passports in a piece of property belonging to him, and they are optimistic about connecting it to an unsolved crime. My brother, he won't have been surprised at what was found in the sewing machine drawers. We always did wonder about our father's business activities.

Other fiction by Graham Pryor

Preferred Lies
Origins
Justice
Kaleidoscope
His Orgy of Crime
After Brexit
Salient
Feuilletage
Stranger Than Normal
Make Hay
Pig
Alba Regained

CPSIA information can be obtained
at www.ICGtesting.com
Printed in the USA
LVHW050207220423
745016LV00004B/532